THE MULTIVERSE PROTOCOL

Olivia Whiddon

Contents

CHAPTER 1

S TARTING DATE: 11/03/2022

As Everyone heard the siren, they ran outside quickly to listen to the announcement, that even some had left half naked, but who cared, this was serious.

"GOOD DAY, FELLOW MENIANS

IT IS SAD TO SAY THAT OUR WORLD WHICH WAS CREATED WITH PRIDE AND CARE HAS FALLEN APART. I'VE JUST GOTTEN NEWS THAT THE FOOD AND WATER SYSTEM HAS OFFICIALLY STOPPED, WE DON'T WHY AND WHAT THE CAUSE MAY BE, BUT... IT IS TRUE. WE HOPE THAT OUR SCIENTISTS CAN COME UP WITH A NEW WAY FOR US TO LIVE OUR LIFE NORMAL AGAIN. THANKS FOR LISTENING.

MAY OUR gods BLESS OUR WORLD." Said, Mayor Peter.

After hearing the announcement, everyone gave a big gasp, some starting crying and others started running straight back home. It was the hardest time the MENIANS had gone through. It was worse when the government decided that they would be taking the food and selling a portion of food back to them so the Scientist would experiment with the rest. And as they were checking the record for the citizen who bought the most groceries in the world, it all came down to Ethan's mom, Angelina

As soon as she had got in the house, she instructed Ethan to go in the room with the food she started piling up from his stomach to his head. 'Mommy, what are you doing?' he asked, worried if his mother had gone crazy. 'Sweetie you're 6, you wouldn't understand, now do what mommy says and get to taking the foods to your room.' 'Yes mommy.' said Ethan as he walked up grumpy. Before you knew it, it was too late, the soldiers which the government asked to search each citizen's house. 'Mrs. Reddy, open the door now.' 'Why?' 'Haven't you heard, the world is running out of food and water and we're trying to recover that.' 'Why are you coming to my house.' 'Mrs. Reddy, we know you're the only person in the entire world to buy a month's grocery of $25 000.' 'So?' 'We just want the food and we'll leave you alone.' 'Then what am I going to eat.' 'We'll give you your money back, and then you'll buy your food back.' 'Mm... Okay.' 'Please open the door.' said the soldier, but no reply.' 'Hello?, Mrs. Reddy?' as said yet again no response. 'I-I think she fled.' 'You think, fuck, George open the damn door.' 'Yes sir.' said George as he ran with a glue stick and somehow broke the door down.

As Angelina heard them enter, she quickly told her son the last words before it was the end for her. 'Listen, you keep on running no matter what, you hear me, you keep on running don't stop, this food is enough to keep you alive, as soon as they stop this, you'll be fine, sweetie I trust you, I know you can do this without me' 'But, Mommy.' 'You got this, I know for a fact.' 'Okay.' 'Remember, what did I say, keep on running, if the coast is clear, you stop and chillax,

I'm relying on you.' said his Mom. 'Okay mommy.' said Ethan. The soldiers were already halfway as they yelled, 'We're coming up.'

Angelina quickly sat the chip which contained all the food and sat it in his front pocket and told him to jump off the window. 'I love you, Mommy.' 'I love you too baby, now jump and don't stop running.' 'Yes, mommy.' said Ethan as he jumped out the back window and made a run for it.

Just as he made it, the soldiers had already made it upstairs and banged the down. 'You know, you could've knocked.' 'Listen here, Angelina, we're tired of your freaking games, where's the food?' 'Gone, with my son.' said Angelina. In anger, the soldier slapped Angelina on her face and she turned back have him a kick sending across the wall. 'Let's do this, bitches.' said Angelina as she quickly ran to the other bodyguard and hit him with the glass picture frame, which had the picture of Ethan and his dad. She then soon jumped on her cardboard and jumped off landing on the other soldier as she picked up his gun and shot the other through his forehead. 'This is so fun.' said Angelina as she started shooting the guys coming from behind

As she tried to shoot the two guys left, the gun was out of bullets and when she tried to kick them, they caught her leg and twisted as the other one pointed the gun at her head and shot her and at that moment, it was the end for Angelina and a new beginning for Ethan.

As Dr Robinson packed his equipment and got ready for work, he too was shocked to hear what had happened to the world, and somehow it has given him an idea on how to save the world. In sonic speed, Robin quickly ran to his car and drove to M.E.N.S.I.O.N where he worked, till date no one knows what it stands for, not even the people who worked there. As drove past his usual road, it was then when he saw almost 15 000 people full of starvation, even begging him as he passed not for money but for food and water. He knew as soon as he got to work he would be honored and help these people.

When he arrived, there was a crowd of reporters waiting to be answered on a way to help the world. 'Ah, Dr Robinson, do you have a solution on how to save Menia, our world.' 'Indeed, I do.' 'Really, what is your solution.' said the news reporter as she broadcast the whole interview to the world. 'You see, we are not the only planet, nor universe nor dimension, I already gathered the equipment to create a portal, which will not only transport us to other universes but also create or clone the item I bring from the Universe, and it will need the help from my co-workers.' 'Wow, you're amazing Dr Robinson, you created the inevitable.' 'Let's just hope it works.' 'Of course, it will.' shouted the reporters as they danced in hope.

When Robin entered the building, it was not long before his co-workers started piling up around him begging him. 'Robin, please can I work with you.' 'Ladies and Gentle███, please, in order to create these portal's I need all of your help, we at least have to make a big one.' 'He's right, we need to help each other, what are we waiting for, let's get to it.' 'Yeah!!!' cheered the whole office of scientists.

It took 15 hours of teamwork, determination, dedication and hard work, but they finally build it, there it was, the first-ever portal they had created.

███████;

It was time, for the creator of the portal to enter it and check if there is a planet, universe, or dimension, that had the resources they needed. As he took a step forward, in an instant he was absorbed into the portal on his adventure.

5 years later

Once again for the second time, the siren went off and it was time for another announcement.

"FELLOW MENIANS,

IT IS SAD TO SAY THAT ON A ADVENTURE TO SEEK FOOD AND WATER FOR US, DR ROBIN ROBINSON DIDN'T MAKE IT BACK, WE HOPE THAT OUR SCIENTISTS ARE ON THE CASE OF PROVIDING FOOD FOR US FOR I HAVE SEEN A LARGE NUMBER OF PEOPLE BEGGING IN THE STREETS.

MAY OUR MEN BLESS OUR WORLD.GOODBYE." Said Mayor Peter as he left in a helicopter.

All hope is gone, what they thought they had is gone. And the begging will therefore continue.

6 YEARS LATER

It was hard for the MENIANS, already half the population of the world has already been depleted. And no matter how much the M.E.N.S.I.O.N tried to stop the cause of starvation, it just didn't work, until one dangerous moment.

When the Scientist had thought that one of the people they sent through the portal actually found food and water, they were wrong. When the portal opened, they heard a noise, like a cat and a dog meowing and barking at the same time. 'Uh... I think you should close the portal, NOW!' 'No, wait, it might be Jefferson.' 'If you don't close it now, we might die.' 'Wait, I see a shadow.' said the Scientist and in a blink of an eye, a creature jumped through the portal and bit the scientist's head off. 'Oh-My-Gosh, RUNNN!!!' Yelled Stanley. As the other scientist tried to run, they didn't make it and before you knew it, a thousand monsters came running out the portal killing every person there was in the room. Soon the monsters began to multiply each destroying mankind, at that moment, Menia was ruined.

The head of M.E.N.S.I.O.N Quickly called the rest of the workers to the main building which had a force shield around it to protect the creatures from entering the building.

"I have come to talk to you guys, that there is no hope for our world, but only one. We've created different kinds of abilities that will give a Menia power in order to save our world. There has been a discovery of Dr Robinson, in a planet which we don't know or never heard of, but we know exists. Fellow colleagues, I'm giving you your final task for your life, since there might not be a life. Each of you have been given a name, you guys will go on a hunt to find these people and bring them back A.S.A.P, They are the only hope our world has.

Once they are found, they will be given their abilities and will be called, THE DIMENSIONS. The reason why we call them this, is because they are a group formed from our establishment, which is the eight letters after di, and the reason why we added, di, is because when saying the word fast, THE MENSIONS, It states DIMENSIONS. I give you all hope and blessings that you find these pupils, for if you do not, the world will suffer, you have 4 days to go. I suggest you get going." Said the head of the M.E.N.S.I.O.N.

CHAPTER 2

E than;

    The Scientist kept on searching for Ethan until they had found him, near a quiet place. 'Mr. Reddy, do you know how far we have looked for you.' 'I'm sorry, who the fuck are you?' 'We are the Scientist that work in the M.E.N.S.I.O.N, and we have been assigned to bring you back to our headquarters.' 'Oh, I'm fine.' 'We're not asking you, we're telling you.' 'Are you forcing me, while the world is suffering from bullshit?' 'I'm afraid so, so don't make us force you.' said one of the Scientists. 'Fine, but I'll need you to close your eyes because I wanna change my clothes.' 'Urgh, fine.' annoyingly said the Scientist. Blinded by what he had said, when they counted to the count of three and opened their eyes, he was gone. 'You have got to be kidding me.' 'We are... Dead!' said the Scientist.

    Clementine;

    As the second group of Scientists was looking for Clementine, they have seemed to find something weird. 'Hello, is anybody there?' 'Grrrrr...!' 'We have lasers.' said one of the Scientists as they were shaking. As it got closer and closer, they quickly took out their guns and prepared to shoot. As it got closer, closer, and closer. With an instant jump, they caught it by its head and were hoping to kill it, but then they saw a girl with hair that had been burnt and what they thought was a lizard's skin around her body. 'Uh, are you Clementine?' 'Whos askin'?' 'Uh, us.' 'What do you want and can please take this helmet off me, NOW!' 'Yes, we are here to ask you if you were willing to come to our headquarters called, M.E.N.S.I.O.N.' 'What's in it for me.' 'You'll get superpowers.' 'Nah, I don't believe in that stuff anymore.' 'Listen, if you don't comprehend, we will be forced to take you there.' 'Nah, my life is crazy now, so, I'll come.' 'Thank Men, because you are very scary.' 'Roar!' roared Clementine as she scared the Scientist.

Aries;

As they searched this weird tropical island, they heard something moving and when they looked up in the sky, they saw a cougar and quickly ran. As they were running, soon a range of cougars started chasing after them. As they tried to turn, one of the cougars bit one of the scientists' heads off, leaving him for bait. You see with these cougars, they didn't care if there was food they could eat, they wanted more, so the rest of the range chased after them. When the scientist thought it was the end for them, someone came flying from the sky. 'Ha-ya!' yelled the child. She quickly stood up and burned his stick which he used to make the carnivores go away. Then she soon burned the whole tree to show the sign that they shouldn't come here. 'Are-Are you Aries?' 'Yes, who you lookin for?' 'We were hoping if you'd come along with us to our headquarters, so we can give you powers.' 'What kind of powers?' 'The greatest of them all.' 'Will I be able to kill other cougars.' 'Definitely.' 'Then count me in.' said Aries as he jumped the vehicle and they drove off.

Thomas;

When the Scientist arrived, they saw an abandoned place but it looked okay, you could say that. When they tried to knock, the door fell. 'Uh... Hello?, Is there anybody here?' asked one of the scientists. No response.They soon went up the stairs hoping they'd find someone, but there were a bunch of rats that were covering something. When they sprayed the rats, they saw a child with blue, black, and red hair. 'Uh, Are you Thomas?' 'Who's asking?' sobbed the little boy. 'We have been sent by our establishment to get people like you, who will be given a special gift.' 'Will there be food?' 'Of course?' 'Then I'll come, I don't have that much company and I never had anyone in my life.' 'We're really sorry, how'd you survive here?' 'I used the rats to make me smell like I am dead.' 'Oh, well, now if you come with us, all that nonsense will fade away.' 'Oh-okay.' 'Good.' said the scientist as he carried the scared and worried little boy to the vehicle and drove off.

Scott;

Now the last Dimension remaining, Scott. There was something about this boy that no one understood, especially the way he operated. When the last group of Scientists searched the house Scott lived in, they found him quickly. 'Wow, that was quick.' 'Hey Scott, you're coming with us.' said one of the scientists. When they tried to grab him by his arm, he somehow twisted it and turned off the lights. 'Oh shit, we have a good one.' 'Prepare your weapons.' said the scientist. Out of nowhere, Scott jumped on one of them and quickly picked the weapon, blasting the lasers and each of them. As he saw they were weak, he quickly ran up to the geyser and blasted it about 7 times. When one of the scientists saw him run out the door, they knew something was suspicious and they warned the rest of the staff to run and before they made it for the door, the house exploded, sending the scientists to fly into mid-air. 'So?, Did you want to give me special powers?' 'Oh you're good!' said the Scientist

M.E.N.S.I.O.N;

When all the groups of Scientists had entered the room with their Dimension, it was tough for the first group who had to why Ethan.

'May I ask why you do not have your Dimension.''Sir, he managed to run away.''And you let him.''No, he-he fooled us.''Wow, just what I needed to hear.'

'Hey, who do think they're talking about.' 'Don't know, never cared.' 'Hey you bozos, concentrate.' 'I'm sorry, who are you calling bozo?''You guys of course.''You wanna get down, homie.''Yeah sure, I could use a beating.'

'HEY!, his right, you should be concentrating, these are important for what I'm about to say.'

"Right,

You four are here today because you guys are the ones who are going to save our planet, I'm sure you asking why?... Simple really, when we checked each child in the world, there were a huge amount of acceptable numbers, but you guys were important. The powers which we will be giving you is greater than any other power in the world.''So?''So... You will be given the ability according to your skills and what you can do, I will remind you that you guys are really important, and if we were to lose you guys, the whole world of Menia would be in danger. Your scientists will now escort you to your room until we found one of you that is missing.' 'Permission to leave sir?' 'Granted.' 'Thank you, sir.' said the Scientists as they went with their Dimension.

It was hard searching for Ethan, but they finally found him. 'Mr. Reddy, we don't have time for fun and games, please will you just come with us to base.' said the female scientist. As Ethan turned around, he was found holding a grenade, ready to throw it. 'Woah, Ethan you need to relax.' 'I lost my mother and now all you have to say is, come with us to base.' 'Mr. Reddy, we know it's tough, but this might help you.' 'Fuck no!, I'm tired of what's happening to our world.' 'Don't you think we are too?' 'No, that's why I'm going to throw this grenade at y'all.' 'Ethan, if you come back to base with us, you can save a lot of lives.' 'How?' 'You've been chosen among four other kids to travel the galaxy and find Robin Robinson, so he can close the portals and stop the creatures from destroying our world.' 'Why me?' 'We don't know, yet, but once we are told, I will notify you.' 'Okay.' 'So please, put the grenade down and let us take you back to headquarters.' 'I wanna keep the grenade unless y'all do something bullshit.' 'If you feel that's safe, then fine.' 'Good, now let's get in the car.' said the scientist.

It was time for the transfer of abilities to the Dimension, But Ethan wasn't there yet.

"Okay,

You will now put your hand over your color or symbol, you're scientists gave you, Dimensions, please move forward." Said the head of the M.E.N.S.I.O.N.'

As they positioned their hands on top of their color or symbol, I didn't work.

'It seems without the fifth dimension, the machine won't work. I'm so-' leaving the head of M.E.N.S.I.O.N to not finish his words, Ethan comes running through. 'I'm here, I'm here!' yelled Ethan, as he stood in front of his color.

There were 5 colors;

WHITE: ETHAN REDDY

BLUE: THOMAS ARMSTRONG

BLACK: ARIES PILLERMAN

RED: CLEMENTINE VALENTINE

GREEN: SCOTT MILLER

It was time for the Dimensions to stand in front of their color and sat their hands on top. In an instant, the machine scanned their hands and blasted power that made each of them, fly through the room.

PREVIEW;

"You now, must of felt something electric go through your body, it's it.

I'm going to describe your powers to you;

WHITE; YOU CONTROL LIGHT AND PEOPLE AND CREATURES, YOU CAN EVEN LIGHT UP A ROOM BRIGHTER THAN THE SUN.

BLUE; YOU HAVE SONIC SPEED, YOU ARE SO FAST, THAT YOU'RE SUPERSONIC, FASTER THAN SOUND. YOU CAN ALSO CREATE ELECTRICITY.

BLACK; YOU ARE DARKNESS, YOU CAN MAKE PEOPLE SEE DARKNESS AND ALMOST LIKE WHITE, YOU CAN MAKE THE WHOLE ROOM DARK THAT YOU STOP SOUND.

RED; YOU ARE FIRE, YOU CAN BLAST AND HEAT THINGS OF COURSE. LET'S NOT FORGET YOU CAN MAKE FIRE DRAGONS.

LAST BUT NOT LEAST;GREEN; YOU ARE EVERYTHING GROUND. YOU CAN MAKE PLANTS AND ROCKS ECT., DO WHAT YOU WANT, PLUS YOU CAN WORK WITH RED AND MAKE A FIRE-BREATHING DRAGON.

REST ASSURED, YOUR POWERS WILL UNLEASH MORE AND MORE AS YOU CONTINUE ON YOUR QUEST.

PLEASE WILL YOU WAIT FOR ME AT BASE, THANK YOU." Said the head of the M.E.N.S.I.O.N.

When they arrived, there it was. The portal which Dr. Robinson had gone through.

'Here's what's going to happen, you all are going to go through different portals to find Dr. Robinson. He is far from where we are, so there are going to be accomplishments to do to get to the next portal. You guys must work as a team, if you don't, you'll DIE!, You got that?' 'Yes, sir!' yelled the Dimensions.

With a press of a button, the portal opened and was ready to absorb. 'RUN NOW!, BEFORE THE CREATURES COME THROUGH!' Yelled the head of M.E.N.S.I.O.N. They quickly ran and the portal absorbed them, and that is how the Dimensions became THE DIMENSIONS. With a new beginning comes an END!

Chapter 3

As the portal opened, the Dimensions quickly jumped out, landing on a planet that looked, normal. 'We have to get moving, the next portal is 155 Kilometers away.' 'Then let's get moving.' 'I'm the leader, so I tell us what to do, let's go.' said Ethan as Aries rolled her eyes. While they were walking, someone needed a break but Ethan didn't want to approve. 'I need a break.' said Clementine. 'No, we have to get moving.' 'Please, I don't think I'll make it.' 'If we stay here, we'll die, we have to get moving!' 'Hey, cut her some slack.' 'I said no, and that's it.' 'What if we don't listen to you.' 'I'll kill you.' 'Do it, I dare you.' said Scott.

Ethan held a fist, and when he opened it, a huge amount of light went through the whole planet. The other Dimensions started bumping into things for they couldn't see.' I hate to do this, but I'm sorry.' said Ethan. As he tried blasting at them, he started to feel dizzy, and the others too. In a blink of an eye, they fell back where they had begun, not knowing what had happened.

'What the hell?' 'Why are we back here.' 'Did we just go back in time?' 'I don't think so.' 'Ugh, let's just keep on moving.' 'I said

I'm in charge so I give the commands.' 'Do you wanna fight Ethan, because I will.' 'Bring it, you little piece of shit.' said Ethan. Aries charged at him, holding a ball of fire. Before she could attack him, again they fell dizzy and went back to where they were.

'Oh come on.' 'Damn it.' 'Wait, I think when we talk a lot, it takes us back.' 'His right.' 'So let's just shut up, even you Ethan.' 'Ugh, fine.' said Ethan with disgust.

They had already walked 56 kilometers and kept their mouths shut, not for long. While Aries was walking, Something slapped Scott making him believe it was Aries. When he turned, they just looked at each other and continued. The second time, something slapped Scott and kicked him in between his legs, and he got pissed. 'What the heck Aries, you wanna kiss or something?' 'What, No.' 'Then stop slapping me, jeez.' 'I didn't slap you.' 'So now you're calling me a liar.' 'Hey Scott, keep quiet, we're almost there.' 'Wait, I wanna know why Aries is calling me a liar.' 'For the last time, I didn't slap you!' Aries said as she blasted Scott leaving for him to fly across the tree. He quickly stood up and made the ground absorb her. Before Aries could attack back, once again, they fell dizzy and went back to where they started.

'Urgh! Urgh! Urgh!' 'Thanks, guys.' 'Your Welcome.' 'Somethings not right.' 'What do you mean?' 'Aries and Scott spoke for about ten minutes and only when they fought did we come back.' 'Yeah, it's like every time we fight, we come back here, in a loop.' 'So we should stop fighting.' 'Yeah, let's go.' 'Hey, if we are powerful, can't we fly?' 'Unfortunately, not,' Said Clementine as they kept walking. While walking, Clementine cheered as she saw the portal and before she knew it, they were dizzy and fell.

'I can't do this anymore, I wanna go home.' sobbed Thomas. 'Hey, maybe it's not us fighting but for us getting to know each other.' 'She's right, we're gonna be working as a team for a long time so, Let's do it.'

'Okay, Hi I'm Ethan, I lost my mother, my dad abandoned me and my mom, she too worked for the M.E.N.S.I.O.N, She would always spoil me, I miss her a lot, that's the reason why I'm doing this so I can help others not to lose their mother, by the way, I'm 17.'

'Hi, I'm Clementine, I was abandoned by my parents and they left me at this weird place where I had to live my life.'

'Hi, I'm Aries, I'm 16 years old, I grew up in a weird environment where I had to learn to fight for food and here I am the fire Dimension ready to help our world.'

'Hi, I'm Thomas, I was abandoned too but in this case, my parents left me with my grandmother who died when I was three, and had to learn how to communicate with rats. I had no one and I'm thankful I was chosen.'

'Sup Assholes, I'm Scott, the hell will I ever tell you my age.' 'Your 17 years.' 'Damn!, Well, I love people, I had a change of heart and I soon realized that I'm... into the same sex. Yeah, you wanna be homophobic, I'll show you, that's all you need to know motherfuckers.' 'Are you like that because you're afraid people will judge you.' 'No... Yeah.' 'Don't worry, we're here for you, I'm sure none of us is homophobic.' 'Nope.' they all said, as Scott thanked them.

As they stood up to continue their journey, Scott quickly interrupted Thomas. 'Hey, why do I feel like you're hiding something.' 'Me, what could I possibly be hiding.' 'Do...You...Also...Like...Guys?' 'What, No.' 'Oh-okay.' said Scott. 'Sorry.' said Scott as he kissed

Thomas on his cheek, which made him blush. While the girls were walking, one of them too had a crush. 'I knew it.' said Clementine. 'What?' 'You like Ethan.' 'WHAT!?' She yelled as everyone looked at her. 'Wow, we're almost there.' Said Aries. 'What are you talking about, I don't like Ethan.' 'You do, I know it for a fact. 'So what if I do, what you gonna do about it?' 'Uhhh, Slap you.' 'Huh?' 'I will if you don't confess it to him.' 'No please don't, I can't let him know yet.' 'Better hurry up.' said Clementine.

While they were walking, they started to feel dizzy again. 'Oh come on.' Said Ethan as he fell, before he could touch the ground, he held onto the tree and he stopped feeling dizzy and saw how his friends disappeared. In shock, he let go and fell back to where they had started. 'Oh come on.' 'I found a way to make it out.' 'What are saying?' 'Before I fell, I held onto a tree where I stopped feeling dizzy and I saw how you guys disappeared.' 'Really?' 'Yes, we just have to make sure when it happens, we hold onto a tree.' 'Then let's go.' said Aries.

While they were at least 100 kilometers away, it began, but they were prepared. 'Now!' yelled Ethan. It worked, when they held on, it stopped and they kept on moving. Before they reached the end, out of nowhere, this huge monster that was made out of loops, jumped out. 'Roar!!' he roared. 'What the?' Thomas said.

'No one ever leaves this planet, but you guys are close, how did you do it, did you figure out the tree.' 'Listen, we don't have time for games, we have a quest to complete.' 'Not on my watch.' said the monster as he made them dizzy, they held on to a tree as Scott got ready to attack. 'Wait, please just let us go, we didn't want to come here.' 'So now you're saying this planet is worth living here.' 'Uh yeah, who would love to repeat what had happened a thousand times.' 'I would.' 'Really Clementine, now's not the right time.' 'Please, sir.' 'Uhhhh, let me see, NOPE!' 'That's it, do your thing, Scott.' 'With pleasure.' said Scott as he made the trees stretch to the monster. 'Scott needs our help, Dimensions assemble.' commanded Ethan as they all stood in a straight line. 'You follow what I say, Scott sends a tree towards as Aries lights it up on fire.' 'And, NOW!' Yelled Ethan. Scott jumped on the tree as it went all the way to the monster, while Aries blasted a huge amount of fire letting the tree on fire. 'Yahhh!' charged Scott to the monster, as soon as got to the monster, it started to burn. 'You guys are stupids.' the monster said as he took them back the way they started.

'Scott needs our help, Dimensions assemble, wait, he took us back.' 'Yeah, we have to outsmart him.' 'There has to be a way, ah, of course.' said Ethan. 'Dimensions, assemble.' he yelled. When Ethan opened his hand, Thomas quickly ran around the monster with a branch that Scott had provided. Before Thomas threw the sharp branch at the monster, Aries lit it on fire and then Thomas let it go. When Ethan took away the light, the monster was tied up while he was burning, guess Thomas was too quick. 'Well done, Dimensions.' 'Yeah, we the boss.' Aries shouted as they laughed with her.

Soon the next portal opened as the Dimensions got prepared to leave. 'Remember guys, we do it as a team.' 'She's right, never leave a Dimension behind, got that?' 'Yes, Ethan.' 'Then let's go.' they yelled while running through the portal.

Chapter 4

As soon as they landed on the new planet, it was just the same as the previous one. 'Oh come on, how'd he do that.' 'Guess his really smart.' 'Ugh, this is the worst.' said Aries. While they were walking, Clementine heard something. 'Did you guys hear that?' 'No, why?' 'I swear I heard something, like a zombie.' 'Hey, that must be your new power.' 'Hey, this is serious, somethings are coming.' said Aries. When they all turned back, there it was, a large herd of zombies, But that wasn't it, these Zombies ran faster than a Dimension.

The Dimensions soon picked up the pace, because the zombies were about 5 000 of them. Clementine soon saw a place where they could hide and directed them there. 'Guys, over here.' She yelled. When they got in, it seemed they left Scott behind and the zombies were halfway. Before they could grab Scott, Thomas ran as quick as possible to get him and bring him back to the factory where he quickly locked the doors. These were the toughest creatures they fought.

They soon got hungry and the zombies kept on piling up in front of the doors. 'What are we going to do?' asked Aries. 'All we can do is sleep until the morning, I promise I'll find us a way to get food, for now, let's rest.' said Ethan.

While they were sleeping, Ethan stood up and his eyes opened up, but started to shine a bright light, what was happening now, was Ethan's new power. He soon saw himself standing in front of a thousand zombies, when the zombies were close to biting him, he saw Aries let a huge amount of fire at the zombies, leaving for them to burn. Then, in a couple of minutes, he woke up breathing hard as he tried to calm down. Soon, it woke up Clementine, who got worried. 'Are you okay?' 'Yeah, I've just been a little over my head lately.' 'Don't worry, we'll find a way.' 'Yeah.' Said Clementine as she fell asleep on Ethan's lap.

It was in the morning, and the blood-thirsty zombies were still waiting outside. Ethan kept on worrying and the dimension's powers were fading away. Ethan knew the only way to get the food was to leave the place they were this instant.

'I say we make a run for it.' 'Are you crazy?' 'Listen, we are losing our powers and... We can die.' 'I'm with Ethan, we have no choice.' 'Fine, let's do it.' Said Aries. They were ready as Ethan took a countdown from 3... 2... 1.

When they ran out, the zombies were somehow standing straight, it seems they were hibernating. So, the Dimensions took it slow and walked all the way to the nearest supermarket. When the Dimensions arrived, they threw everything across and started eating literally anything, while Ethan took a bite of a chocolate cake. 'You have got to be kidding me, why would you only eat a piece of cake?' 'I don't want to eat a lot after running away from fast zombies, you know what, they shouldn't be called fast zombies but Speedos.' 'Wow, what a name.' 'Yeah, whatever.' said Ethan as he walked away.

While Thomas was looking through the freezers for a fizzy drink, he saw one of the freezers shaking and moving. 'Uh... Guys, you have to come see this.' said Thomas. When they arrived, Clementine got so scared, that she made the room dark. 'Uh, Clemy, please take away your darkness.' 'I can't, I'm too scared.' 'Well, that doesn't help at all.' said Aries, soon the freezer which had been shaking had opened, but they couldn't see who it was for Clementine made it dark. 'Shit!, Uh, Clementine, this would be the right time to take away the darkness.' 'I-I can't.' said Clementine as she ran.

Then it began, the zombies came running out of the freezer heading for the dimensions, as they picked up their shoes and ran.

PREVIEW:

The Dimensions ran for their life, as soon as they got to the door, one of the speedos had bitten off Thomas's kneecap. 'Ahhhh!' he yelled. Soon Scott heard his scream and made the ground absorb everything, including the zombies. As soon as Scott got Thomas's hand, Clementine stopped feeling scared thanks to Aries and the darkness went away. When they looked at the hole, Scott created, soon the speedos jumped out like they were kangaroos. 'What the heck are these things?' asked Scott. Scott quickly signaled the roots underground to carry Thomas as they ran. As soon as Aries saw these creatures, naked, she instantly puked. Because she had fire powers, along with the vomit, fire came out and burned the speedos. She quickly stood up and ran.

When they arrived at the factory, they quickly closed the doors as Scott made the roots surround the doors. 'What the hell was that,

Clementine?' 'I'm sorry, I didn't mean to, I freaked out.' 'Well, that doesn't help out at all.' 'We could've died.' 'I'm sorry.' 'Sorry doesn't fix anything you piece of shit.' 'Okay, come done Aries, if get too upset you'll burn down this whole place.' 'I-I'm sorry, I'm going to go sleep, I'm very tired.' said Aries as she left with a sigh. With a sad emotion, Clementine soon cried and made the whole room dark. 'Well, this means it's bedtime, goodnight guys.' said Ethan.

While Scott was healing the bite the Speedos took, Thomas got a hard-on. 'Oh-my-Gosh, you're hard.' 'I don't know what it is, I just, don't know.' 'Thomas, when you saved me, I felt something.' 'What?' 'You held me very tight like you were going to lose me.' 'I-I didn't want to lose you.' 'Awe, that's sweet.' 'Shut up and heal my wound.' said Thomas as Scott laughed, love was blooming in the air. Soon Scott got curious and finally asked Thomas what he was waiting so long to ask. 'Thomas, do you-' before he could finish, Ethan woke up and started breathing hard, demanding that the dimensions left.

'Ethan, what the fuck is wrong with you?' 'We need to go, now.' 'It is the middle of the night, you better go to sleep or else so help me I'll make Aries blast you.' 'Please, you have to believe me, we can't stay here.' begged Ethan. Soon Clementine heard something, as she looked up, Ethan knew she knew. 'That's why we have to go, you hear them, we'll die.' 'He's right, we have to go.' 'Fuck no, I'm tired.' 'Aries, if we stay here, we'll die.' said Clementine. Soon the roof started to shake and Ethan had enough. 'Clementine, make this room DARK.' Said Ethan as Clementine made the room dark. Because they couldn't see, they had no choice but to go out, so Aries, Thomas, and Scott ran as quickly as they could, as soon as they all got outside, they all saw the speedos a.k.a fast zombies on the roof. As Ethan's vision predicted, the roof fell leaving the whole factory to explode.

The whole Dimensions hearts were beating hard, they were so scared. 'Let's get moving, there has to be a place to spend a night.' 'I hope.' said Aries. While they were walking, they saw dogs running away from where they were heading. They soon stared at each other but with nervousness. 'I don't think this direction is safe.' said Thomas. Soon Clementine heard something, angry and boy, it was hungry. She soon told the Dimensions that they find another path, but it was too late.

When they turned around, there was this huge creator with the sharpest teeth they had ever seen, and it looked like it could devour the Dimensions in one bite. They had nowhere to go but fight. Soon the speedo started to scream, alerting the other speedos to come. In a blink of an eye, it charged at them ready to eat. As always, Ethan yelled 'DIMENSIONS ASSEMBLE!' and the Dimensions powers would activate ready for battle. Soon Scott made the trees fall leaving for the Speedo to fall to the ground, as Ethan sent light to it leaving it to be blind. As the Speedo stood up, Aries tried to blast it but then the others had arrived and they were running faster than before they could. The shocking part made the Dimensions very nervous. Soon the speedos had wings coming out of them, as they started to fly. And right behind the Speedos, the portal to the next planet had opened. They knew that they had to fight all of them to get free.

Without hesitation, Scott sent rock monsters for the Speedos as they took half of them. Ethan quickly sends a hot beam of light burning the Speedos in the middle of their body. Clementine heard one of the dogs running back as she communicated to them and the dogs went attacking. So far they did good, until one of the Speedos grabbed Thomas and went to feed him to the giant Speedo. 'Ethan, Scott, they took Thomas.' yelled Clementine. With Anger, Scott made all the rocks head for the speedo that took Thomas and by his anger, he forgot Thomas couldn't walk as he started falling and the other Speedos were running and flying toward Thomas. When Scott tried to get to him, one Speedo got him and they started battling. It was only Ethan as Aries and Clementine were helping out Scott. And at that moment, Ethan's vision was going to come true.

As he ran to catch Thomas, he blinded the speedos while he caught Thomas, when he removed the light, all of the speedos came flying toward him. In fear, Ethan somehow unlocked a new ability. He made a sword out of his powers which he used to fight the Speedos. When he was almost finished, the giant speedo took his sword and broke it, while he carried Ethan and twisted his ankle. 'Ahh!' yelled Ethan. As the other Dimensions tried to help Ethan, their powers faded away. 'What are we going to do?' 'What can we do?' asked Clementine.

The Dimensions were shaking with fear, while the Speedo held Ethan ready for a big meal. It was at that moment, that the love of Ethan made Aries unlock her new ability. As Aries held her hand in a circular motion, a huge hot fireball appeared, and in Less than a minute, she threw the fireball aiming for the gaint. When it hit the gaint, there was this huge explosion, everything around them went flying and as all the Speedos and the giant Speedo disappeared into dust. As Ethan landed on the ground, Aries was the first one to run to him. 'I think we should go to?' 'No, it's their moment, wait, I hear people?' 'Really?' said Scott as he left with Thomas and Clementine.

'Ethan, are you okay?' 'Yeah, yeah I'm fine.' 'Oh, thank God.' 'Thanks, Aries.' Said Ethan as he held Aries's hand, which made her blush. As I said, love was blooming in the air. While they had their time, the others brang people who have been hiding for years away from the Speedos. 'Guys, you won't believe how many people we found?' 'How many?' 'About 50 000.' 'We can help build their town back.' 'We have like three hours until the portal disappears.' 'Cool.' said Ethan.

They soon help out as Scott used the tress to regrow and make wood while building the houses. Aries used the iron they found to make weapons for them. Thomas was the one to build the houses, of course, his leg was healed thanks to Scott. Clementine used her healing powers to find all the animals and brought them back. While Ethan used his sword to train them how to fight.

It was finally over and the Dimensions had ten minutes until the portal disappeared. Although, Ethan had a question that had to be answered. 'I would just like to ask you one question please, how were those zombies created?' 'All we know, it has something to do with Scientists.' 'Mmm... Thanks, we'll see you guys next time.' 'Goodbye.' they waved as they wishes them away.

Before Ethan entered the portal, he had the worst vision. As soon as the vision was finished, he stood there more scaredly than ever. You see what had happened now was... Ethan knew how all of this would end, meaning, HE SAW THE END!

Chapter 5

As they entered this weird but normal planet, Ethan felt weak and slipped. 'Ethan, are you okay?' asked Aries but no reply. Scott then picked him up and headed for the closest house that they could relax in. Just as they were about to enter this weird house, some people pulled them into this huge house.

'Hey, what the heck?' 'You must be new.' 'What?' 'Do you even know where you are?' 'No, but I know where I can put you.' said Aries as she held a fist. 'Ha, ha, ha, she's joking, please, tell me where we are?' 'This is Errormas, this planet is sick, whilst you are walking, anybody can kidnap you plus the most powerful thief here is Dulshe, he is swift as sound, he can steal from you without you knowing.' 'So, what's the damn reason why you brang us here?' 'Can you stop being so rude?' 'I don't know, can I?' 'I swear Aries, there's never a stop button on you.' said Clementine as she left.

As they got into this huge room which had about eight beds, Aries quickly ran and jumped on one of them, as Clementine sighed. As Scott dropped Ethan on one of the beds, Thomas quickly pulled Scott's arm as they headed for the balcony.

'What's wrong?' 'What do you think happened with Ethan?' 'I guess he's going through a lot.' 'I hope he wakes up.' 'Why did you really bring me here?' 'Well, I wanted to ask you something important?' 'Really?, I wanted to ask you something too.' 'Okay, I'll go first, Will you be... Able to ask Clementine if she has feelings for me?' asked Thomas. After hearing that, Scott got upset and accidentally made a tree grow in the middle of the house. Scott then quickly ran straight to the bedroom while the owners of the house were yelling.

'Are you sure we should let them live here?' 'They'll die if they go out there, it's not like they have superpowers or anything.' 'Urgh, whatever.' said the owner's wife as she walked away, while he looked up with regret.

While they were sleeping, Ethan had another vision, and once again it was about THE END. He then woke up and started breathing hard, as everyone woke up. 'Ethan are you okay?' 'No, I just need to take a breather, I'm going outside.' said Ethan as he walked to the backyard and just stood there. 'He needs someone to talk to him.' 'Hey, Aries, why don't you go?' 'Uh, no.' 'Urgh fine, I'll go.' said Clementine as she stood up and left.

When she got there, she saw Ethan crying. 'Ethan, what's wrong?' 'My new powers a curse.' 'What do you mean?' 'Let's say you can see what's going to happen right, but, you see something you don't want to see.' 'Is that how you knew the roof was going to collapse?' 'Yes.' 'May I ask, what did you see?' 'Uh...' Ethan began to freeze, as once again he saw another part of the end. When the vision ended, he stood up and ran to the bedroom while Clementine yelled out his name calling out for him.

As a new day approached them, Ethan was once again, out. The others soon got ready as the owners of the house, told them if they wanted to stay they had to do what the owners asked. 'Are you sure you'll survive out there, you know you can just order food?' 'No it's fine, the four of us will get the things required, right guys?' 'Yeah.' the three of them said.

While the four of them were walking, Scott and Thomas got distracted by a play and they left the rest of the group. 'Hey, where are Scott and Thomas?' 'I don't know and I don't care, they have superpowers.' 'Mmmm, you're right, let's keep on moving.' said Clementine.

While they were walking, Clementine saw a sign which said:

DO YOU WANT SOMETHING DESPERATELY, WELL I HAVE THE THING FOR YOU, YOU CAN WISH FOR ANYTHING IN THE UNIVERSE, BUT YOU'LL ONLY GET ONE WISH, BY ONE CONDITION, COME TO THE VISHER STORE AND SAY POPPER, AS THE PASSWORD. I'LL BE WAITING FOR YOU.

After reading the sign, Clementine realised that someone was trying to search her bags. When she turned, there he was, Dulshe. He quickly grabbed Clementine's bag and started jumping roof from the roof and ran quickly whilst Clementine yelled 'THEIF!'

Soon Aries called Thomas and Scott's name, as they arrived at where they were, Aries told Thomas to chase after him while they came up with a plan. You see, no one in this world had powers so it was hard to catch him, but he didn't know that he was messing with the second-fastest person in the universe.

As Thomas got ahead of him, he tripped Dulshe, and he fell from roof to roof when he finally hit the ground, Scott commanded the roots to surround him. When they arrived, Dulshe managed to get out of the roots and when he tried to run, Aries blasted him not from her hands but her eyes, a new ability was unlocked. As they fell, Clementine made his eyes only see darkness, and he started screaming.

'What's wrong, not a fan of the dark?' said Clementine as the four of the Dimensions laughed. When she took the darkness away, he saw himself hanging, whilst the other people who lived in this world came to see, and believe me they were shocked. 'How did you do it?' someone asked. Remember that the Dimensions as superheroes should keep their identity hidden, so they lied and said they were siblings with the same name but with different first letters. 'I'm Anna, she's Sanna, his Danna, and his Wanna.' 'Yep, that's us.' 'Thank you guys so much, you are the very first people to catch Dulshe, not even the police from the other planets could stop him.' 'It was nothing sir, we would just like to know where the Visher store is?' 'Why do you want to go there?' 'For some reason, do you know where it is?' 'Uh yes, down the road, you'll see an abandoned house, and behind it is a shack, that's where he lives.' 'Oh, wow, thank you sir.' said Clementine as she left with the other dimensions.

While they were walking, Thomas wanted to ask Scott desperately to ask Clementine if she has feelings for him. 'Hey Scott, did you ask her?' 'No, and I'm not going too.' 'B-But why not?' 'First of all, why don't you ask her yourself, I'm not your walkie-talkie.' 'I never said you were.' 'So then, go yourself and ask her if she has feelings for her.' 'What's wrong?' 'Nothing.' 'Somethings up, if you don't tell me, I'll break my knee again.' 'Actually, do it, I'd love to break it apart more.' said Scott as he walked away leaving Thomas in Silence.

Before Thomas could speak, Clementine yelled 'WE'RE HERE!' 'Uh, why are we here?' 'Let's just go inside.' 'Urgh, fine.' sighed Aries.

When they entered the place, there was no one. 'Hello?, is there anybody here?' 'I don't think so.' 'Uh, should we go home?' 'Wait, there seems to be a tunnel leading down to an underground area.' 'I'm so going there.' said Aries as she jumped through the hole and the rest of the Dimensions followed her.

When they got there, they saw so many papers and booklets and a weird glass of blue smoke, as Clementine went further, she was pushed by someone who swung through this cave. As Aries saw that, she blasted the rope he was swinging on with her eyes and he fell. Before he could hit the ground, Thomas caught him.

'Who are you people and what are you doing here?' 'Popper.' said Clementine. The man stood in shock and told them to follow him. He led to another cave but bigger, where there was this huge creature behind cages. 'Do you remember the condition you have to do when you want to make a wish, well, I need you guys to fight this monster.' 'Sure we can do this.' 'Yeah, I'm so in the need to fight a monster.' 'Oh yeah and also, when you're done, please will you give me one of his teeth.' 'Uh, Sure.' said Clementine as they prepared.

As the cage opened, the monster moved slowly out and to their surprise, it was very tall. 'Lady's and gentlemen, I give you, THE ERASEMATIC.' Said the guy.

The creature then turned to downsize as he made the dimensions fly across the room. 'This is going to be tough, but we got this guys.' said Clementine as she made the eyes of the creature dark. As Aries jumped high, preparing a huge ball of fire, she somehow felt as if she were losing her powers. As she blasted the creature, it moved a step back as Scott commanded the roots to tie around its neck and force it tall fall down. When Clementine tried to jump on it, aiming a ball of black smoke, it somehow disappeared and the monster managed to grab hold of clementine and throw her across the room. When Aries tried blasting a fireball, the creature held the roots and caught her while it made her hit Thomas and they both aimed for the wall as they both went through it. As Scott tried his best to make a tree grow in the middle of the creature, it took a minute for a new part of the root to grow as the creature held him by his neck and started choking him. Then threw him into the cage bars where he broke his arm. 'AAHH!' cried Scott.

Hearing Scott's cry, Ethan suddenly woke up. 'Are you okay?' asked the owner of the house. 'My friends, where are they?' 'They left out for the store, but I'm sure by now they're dead.' 'No, they can't be dead.' said Ethan as he ran out of the house and headed for his friend's.

When Ethan arrived, there he saw them lying down and the creature was about to step on Aries. Ethan quickly formed his light sword as he shined a huge amount of light into the eyes of the creature leaving for it to start roaming around the room. As it got closer to the wall, Ethan quickly jumped as he cut one of its eyes out and slid down cutting through his stomach and in between his legs.

While the creature was roaring, Ethan told the rest of the Dimensions to get up and as he was about to say the most important word, he gave a little smile and said 'DIMENSIONS ASSEMBLE!' Yelled Ethan. Out of nowhere, each of the Dimensions powers came back, and soon Aries headed at the creature as she sat her fire lasers from her eyes at the creature's face, leaving for it to explode. As the creature was about to fall, Thomas quickly took Ethan's sword and started cutting through it, leaving it into pieces as he grabbed two teeth from the creature.

When it was all over, Ethan then fainted once again, but fear not, because Clementine's plan was about to take place. As she gave the teeth to the guy, he squeezed them where a weird red spit fell in the blue bottle of smoke and turned it white. 'Here you go, whatever you wish for will happen.' 'OMG, why didn't you say so, I have so many things I'd like to wish for.' 'Wait, I actually would like to know something, I think I should have the wish.' 'First of all, none of us is getting the wish, but Ethan.' 'Urgh, why him?' 'Well, Ethan's new power is kinda scary, I realised that he-' before she could finish, Ethan interrupted her. 'I saw how everything was going to end, meaning the Flippin end.' said Ethan as the rest of the Dimensions gasped. 'Woah, I'm kinda scared.' 'But that's why Ethan has been weak, so when I found this guy, I knew that he would want to forget that vision so, Ethan, make the wish.' said Clementine as she gave him the bottle of orange smoke.

As Ethan held the bottle, he knew once he destroyed this bottle and made his wish, he will never remember how it ends, so yeah, he held the glass in the air as he said 'I wish for the visions I've been having these days to fade away.' said Ethan as he dropped the glass. As the glass broke, Ethan's head faced the roof as a huge beam of light reflected on the ceiling. You see what was reflecting, was the end but luckily it was too much light so no one could see it. When the last part of the vision was over, the whole room exploded and the Dimensions and the guy flew into the air and luckily the Dimensions landed safely but the guy didn't, may he R.I.P.

As Ethan stood straight, he felt better. 'So, are you okay?' 'Yep.' said Ethan as the portal opened up. 'Hey look, the next portal.' 'Wait, let's give the people who really help us their products back.' said Clementine.

'Thank you so much for everything, we hope to see you again.' 'Who are you guys really?' 'Just some teens balancing life and power, we better get going, till we meet again.' 'Goodbye.' 'Goodbye.' said Clementine as she and the rest of the Dimensions went through the portal and it closed.

CHAPTER 6

As the dimensions entered their new planet, the portal had left them in mid-air, where they started falling. 'We're going to die.' 'No, we're not.' 'What do you mean.' 'We can't fly.' 'But Scott can help us.' 'Really.' 'Yes, ⊠⊠⊠⊠⊠⊠⊠⊠⊠⊠ ⊠⊠⊠⊠⊠⊠⊠⊠⊠!' Yelled Ethan. Scott then made a tree grow as it produced vines for them to use to land down.

As they entered an abandoned house, everyone settled as Ethan called Aries and Thomas. 'What do you want from us.' 'I need you guys to practise something, I've been studying you guys and I think you guys can create something wonderful.' 'I'm sorry no, I'm not doing this.' 'You have to.' 'Come on, Aries, let's do it.' 'What if I don't want to.' 'Well you have to, I'm the leader and it's a command.' 'Command my ass, bitch.' said Aries as she left. 'I'll leave.' said Thomas.

As Thomas was waking, he then bumped into Scott. 'Oh, hey, I'm sorry.' 'Urgh!' 'What did I ever do to you?' 'Just leave me, the fuck, alone.' said Scott as walked away, while Clementine was heading Thomas's way. 'Oh, Hey Thomas.' 'Hey, Clementine.' 'How are you?'

'I'm great, and you.' 'I'm sad.' 'Oh dear, what's wrong.' 'It's fine.' 'Okay, I better get going, Ethan's calling us.' said Clementine as she left leaving for Thomas's facial expression to be sad.

As Everyone sat down, Aries was pissed. 'Why the fuck did you call this meeting when I was busy.' 'Just wanted to let you know that the next portal is two-hundred and fifty-five kilometres from here.' 'The fuck, that's too far.' 'I know, but that's why I need you and Thomas to do as I say.' 'Why should we be listening to you, no one made you the leader.' 'But I surely know what to do, and you guys need me.' 'The fuck we do.' 'Yes, you do.' 'You know what, fuck off Ethan, go somewhere else while we'll go to the next portal.' 'Only the rest of the group can decide!' 'Sorry Ethan, I think you should go, you don't even know what problems we have.' 'Yeah, you're just bossing us around.' 'You're too vile.' said the Dimensions. 'Ok then, Goodbye.' said Ethan as he left, giving one stare at his friends and left.

As the dimensions were on their way, Aries's hands started to feel hot. 'Wow, my hands are so hot.' 'What do you mean, your powers are fire, you're supposed to be immune to fire.' 'I don't know, it's soo hot.' 'Uh guys, you have to see this.' 'What?' said Clementine. As she, Aries and Scott turned around, they saw dogs which had three heads on one body.

PREVIEW

'Whatever you do, do not move.' 'That's going to be a problem.' 'What do you mean.' 'I have a Fart and I can't hold it.' 'Oh shit.' said Aries as Scott farted. The dogs then moved their heads facing the direction of the Fart and soon saw Aries and the rest of the Dimensions. 'ROAR!' The dogs roared as they ran towards the Dimensions. 'RUN!' Yelled Aries. As Scott, Clementine and Thomas got to cover, Aries got ready to blast them. 'Wait, Aries, don't do that.' said Clementine however she was late as Aries blasted a huge fireball aiming at the dogs. Before the fireball could reach the dogs, the dogs opened their mouths as they let the fireball enter their stomachs. They then prepared to blast Aries, as She stood there shocked. Before the dogs' blasts could reach Aries, Thomas grabbed her and Scott made the ground open apart and the dogs fell in growling. 'Are you stupid, you could get yourself killed.' 'I-I'm sorry.' 'Urgh, Let's go.' said Clementine.

While they were walking, Aries screamed for her life as she caught fire. 'Ahhh, please someone, get water.' 'I'll try.' said Scott. 'What's happening, Aries.' 'I don't know, my whole arm is on fire.' 'Just breath.' 'I can't, it's getting hotter.' 'Hold on.' 'I CAN'T' Yelled Aries as she let a huge amount of fire blast from her mouth while Clementine jumped back in fear.

The fire kept on blasting out of Aries's mouth for about fifty minutes, and Scott was still trying to get water from the ground. 'We should've never let Ethan go, we really need him.' 'No, shhhhut up, we don't neeeeeeed him.' said Aries as she was trying to speak while the fire was blasting from her mouth. 'We have a problem.' 'What is it?' 'My powers are gone.' 'WHAT!' Yelled Clementine.

Soon the ground started to shake as Aries fire went out of her mouth to an area in front of them. As the dimensions stood up, they saw Aries fire grow into a huge and powerful dangerous monster combining from the ground to the clouds, causing thunderstorms and lightning, as it roared and the whole planed had shaken. 'What the fuck is happening!' Yelled Clementine.

PREVIEW¦

As it roared, fire came blasting from its mouth heading straight to Aries as she started to float while the fire was burning on her. Clementine then started to get scared and immediately made the whole planet dark and only the monster and Aries we providing light. 'I miss Ethan, this is all trash.' tearfully said, Scott. 'Yeah I know, ETHAN!' Yelled Clementine.

As they began to look. Aries started to burn so much that her legs and arms started to dust away. 'No, Aries, NO!' Yelled Clementine as Scott held her back from her running to Aries. Before Aries was left with only her face, Ethan appeared and he then blasted a huge light beam at the monster as its head burst off leaving Aries's body parts to appear and for Clementine to make the darkness disappear. 'It's time for some real action, ☒☒☒☒☒☒☒☒☒ ☒☒☒☒☒☒☒☒!' Yelled Ethan. Soon Scott's powers appeared as water burst from the dirt and went straight to the fire monster as he began to burn away, but they couldn't stop him. As everyone's powers came back, Ethan took Aries and Thomas and said,'Listen, I need you guys to do as I say.' 'Fine, please just get this monster away from us.' 'You guys have to hold hands.' 'No way.' 'Are you being stubborn?' 'Sorry.' said Thomas as he held Aries's hand.

Ethan then told them to force all of their powers in between the circle of their hands. As they let go of their hands, their powers combined, in a circular motion.

PREVIEW¦

As their powers finally became one, they both pushed it to the sky at high speed then it burst into this beautiful bird that had half of Thomas and Aries's powers. 'Wow, that is beautiful.' said Aries.

PREVIEW¦

'FIREED, GET THAT BEAST!' Yelled Ethan as the bird-headed straight to the monster folding its wings in the image of a huge powerful ball. Before it could hit the creature, Ethan told Scott to form a shield over them as the bird headed into the creature, causing a huge explosion destroying half of the planet, while Aries's hand created a fire egg.'What the fuck is that?''I think it's an egg, with something inside of it.' 'Woah, that's crazy.' said Thomas, as the egg started to move. 'Open the shield, Scott.' said Ethan as Scott opened the shield.

'We're really sorry Ethan, it's all our fault.' 'It's okay, at least now you know how important I am to you guys, I am the only one who can activate your powers.' said Ethan. As Everyone headed to the next portal, Aries fire-egg started to go crazy. 'Uh guy, I think it's opening, Ahhhh!' Yelled Aries.

CHAPTER 7

S OMEWHERE IN THE UNIVERSE...

'My Lord, I have done what you have asked me to do.' 'Good, now for you to have the powers, you'll need an animal, any kind, if you do not get it, your powers will leave you, do I make myself clear?' 'But Lord, how will I find an animal!' 'Make a plan about it, now, get out.' The Lord said as he left.

While Roxet was walking through the planet, he went to his friend, who could track anything in the universe. 'I need your help.' 'What is it, now?' 'I need you to find me an animal.' 'Cool, let me search.' his friend said. After searching the universe, he found an animal. 'Found it.' 'Really?' 'Indeed, it's by the planet, gromax, which half of it has exploded.' 'What kind of animal?' 'I don't know, it's still going to hatch, but I think it has-.' 'That's enough information, I better get going.' Roxet said as he left, floating with rocks.

Meanwhile...

Aries hand then disappeared as the egg was close to exploding. As it Aires started to float, immediately the egg hatched as a huge explosion appeared and the whole Dimensions fell back. When

Aries stood up, there was a bright light and as it disappeared, there was a beautiful bird that started coughing fire, as it looked at Aries and flew toward her.

PREVIEW;

Aries started to pat it as it blasted a huge fireball out of its mouth. 'Whoa, little buddy.' Aries said. As the rest of the Dimensions came to see, it started to get angry. 'It's okay, they're with us.' Aries said as he flew to them and sniffed them. 'It's beautiful.' Clementine said as she started to cuddle it. After a minute, Aries fainted. 'Oh my God!' Yelled Clementine. 'She must be tired.' Ethan said as he carried her.

While they were walking, Aries woke up in Ethan's hand and was surprised. 'Wha-What happened?' 'Well, I guess after you gave birth, you fainted due to the usage of giving birth.' 'Does this mean I'm a mother?' 'I guess so.' 'Would you like to be the-' before Aries could finish her question, a lot of rocks came from the sky and started hitting the Dimensions, as they flew back leaving Aries's pet to fly across.

When the dust cleared, Aries heard her bird squeak as she ran towards it. When she got to him, somebody was holding him as he took the bird and disappeared. Aries kept on blasting fireballs but she was too late. She then fell to the ground, and she began to cry, fire tears. 'We're sorry, Aries.' Clementine said as she hugged Aries.

As Ethan headed to Aries, he stopped as his eyes turned white. Ethan then saw the bird and the person who took it by a desert, and the kidnapper was holding it captive in a cage made of rocks. As Ethan woke up, he started breathing heavily as the rest of the Dimensions came running. 'Are you okay?' 'I-I think I just had a vision.' 'Whoa, what did you see?' 'I saw your pet with somebody in a desert with one mountain, and it looks like he was going to do something to him.' 'Do you know where I can find him?' 'I don't think-' before Ethan could finish his sentence, his eyes blasted a small light it has a shape of an arrow. 'I think we should follow that thing.' 'Well then, what are we waiting for?' Aries said as the rest of the Dimensions went with her.

While they were walking, it began to become nighttime and the Dimensions were exhausted, so they went into a shelter and went to bed.

While Ethan was sleeping, he then woke up to a white light as it shined on his face. He then started to look around and as he heard a voice whispering to him. 'HELLO?' He yelled. As he kept on walking, the voice got louder. 'Ethan...' The voice whispered. As Ethan got close to the light, he saw it in a human form as it said, 'YOU WILL SEE THE END, ETHAN.' Yelled the voice as it charged at Ethan leaving for him to wake up.

As Ethan woke up, he started to breathe heavily, as Aries woke up and sat next to him. 'What's wrong?' 'I think my visions are haunting me.' 'What makes you say that?' 'I think I just had a vision slash nightmare that I was going to see the end.' 'Don't worry, it'll be alright.' 'I hope so.' 'Let's go back so sleep.' Aries said.

MEANWHILE... 'Master, they are coming for the animal.' 'That's disappointing.' 'What should we do master?' 'Mmm..., send in, Slither, he'll definitely take care of them, get the animal ready.' 'Yes sir.' The servant said.

PRESENT... As the dimensions were continuing their journey, someone whispered by Aries's ear. 'HIS GONE...' The voice whispered as Aries started to look around. Out of nowhere, the Dimensions flew into trees as Ethan yelled, '☒☒☒☒☒☒☒☒☒ ☒☒☒☒☒☒☒☒!'

The Dimensions powers then activated and Aries blasted a huge fireball that displayed and man and a blue shadow of the man.

PREVIEW;

'Who are you?' 'I'm Slither, I've been sent by my master to kill the Dimensions.' Slither said as punched the ground and his shadow morphed into ten more as they started attacking the Dimensions.

Scott then created tree creatures as they charged at the shadows destroying half of them, while slither created more. Soon, two of them held Thomas as he gave a loud scream sending them straight to Slither. 'Aries, blast him.' Ethan Yelled as Aries blasted a huge fireball, aiming at Slither.

Before the fireball could hit slither, Slither then morphed into his shadow form as he appeared in front of Aries and punched her so hard that a scar appeared next to her eye while it started bleeding. Slither then punched her in the face as flew to the ground.

As Ethan saw what had happened, he got upset and created his light beam sword and charged at Slither. As Ethan cut through the chest of Slither, Clementine blinded him with darkness as Scott commanded the vines to tie him up. It was up to Aries and she was too weak. In a shocking event, Thomas ran straight to slither as he passed through him, slither screamed and exploded right in front of them.

As the Dimensions fell to the ground, Ethan ran straight to Aries as he carried her while they continued their quest.

When they arrived, they saw this huge mountain that had a huge door. 'I think we are here?' 'I think so too.' 'Let's get Aries's pet back.' Ethan said.

As they entered the place, it was magical as they passed a waterfall filled with different kinds of water creatures. As Clementine tried to put her hand in the water, a huge flew to her as it hit her hand and she gave a loud scream. 'Clementine, what's wrong?' 'A rock hit me.' Clementine said as more came flying. 'TAKE COVER!' Ethan yelled.

As the rocks stopped coming, someone appeared and dropped the bird in a cage to the ground. 'I need this animal' 'No, you don't.' 'It doesn't matter, if you don't leave, I'll be forced to hurt you.' 'I dare you.' Ethan said. Soon the man created huge monsters out of rocks as Aries woke up. 'XXXXXXXXXX XXXXXXXX!' Ethan Yelled. Clementine then jumped as she blinded them. Scott then touch the ground as huge trees grew right into the rocks. When the creatures fell, they saw the man running outside with the pet. Before the other Dimensions could go after him, Aries stopped them and said, 'I'll take care of him, you just stay here.' as she ran after him.

As Aires saw him, she blasted the cage as it fell to the ground with the bird in it. As the man turned around, Aries saw him as rocks started to levitate around him.

PREVIEW;

Aries then jumped as the rocks came flying straight to her. As she prepared a fireball, the cage was very near to hitting the ground. Aries then blasted it to him as he also blasted his power to her. The clash between them got stronger and Aries was getting weaker. Being disturbed by her bird falling, she lost control and the man rocks overcame her power and blasted her through the mountain.

As the other dimension saw it, they quickly jumped out of the mountain, as Ethan blasted a huge fire beam at the man but he missed as a huge rock went over Ethan. As Ethan tried to hold it, he wasn't strong enough and the rock fell over him as he hit the ground. While Thomas tried to catch the bird, the man flew to him as he punched him and made a rock hit him by his private part, leaving for Thomas to crouch as the man hit his back with his elbow, leaving for Thomas to fall.

As Clementine tried to blind him, the man made the rocks absorb both her hand and her feet. All the Dimensions were defeated and as the cage hit the ground, it opened leaving for the bird to roll on and on. The man then headed to Aries as he kept on punching her, leaving her to bleed more.

As her bird saw this, it started to get angry and then it roared so loud, that he man and Aries turned around as they saw it morph into this bird with fire flames on its wings and its head.

PREVIEW;

'What the?' The man said. Soon the bird came flying straight to the man as it blasted a red-yellow fire from its mouth the man leaving for him fly across, hitting the man's head to the mountain. As the bird tried to snuggle on Aries, the man started moving his hands in a circular motion, letting all the rocks come straight to him. As he sent the rocks into the air, a huge rock monster appeared, roaring so loud that Everyone flew into the mountain.

PREVIEW;

The monster then grabbed the bird as Aries screamed, 'NO!'. The rock monster then started to squeeze the bird in his hand, while Aries kept on yelling and the Man was laughing. Soon, the was a huge light glowing from the hand of the monster, as the monster let go, it was Aries bird, but bigger. This time its wings were full of fire and they were huge.

PREVIEW;

Soon the bird then blasted into the monster as it exploded leaving for the rocks to fall around the planet. The bird then went to the man as the man tried to throw rocks at the bird but they kept on burning away. As the bird passed through the man with its wings, he burned and turned into dust as he flew away while the bird morphed into its normal size.

As the rest of the Dimensions came running to see this amazing bird, Aries somehow got healed. 'This bird is amazing.' 'Yeah, I would want one just like it.' Clementine said as the portal opened. 'Well, let's get going, welcome to the team...?' 'I'll name him, TEACS.' 'Mmm, TEACS, that's a cool name.' 'It's our first letter from each of our names.' 'Welcome to the team, TEACS.' Ethan said as the rest of the Dimensions went through the portal.

MEANWHILE...

'Sir, they are successfully passing planets, they are getting very close to Dr Robinson.' 'Well then, let's get rid of one of them.' Someone said.

CHAPTER 8

She ran for life as five men were chasing after her. She then stopped and when they all surrounded her, she held a fist where green fire flames were lit. As she touched the ground, the fire spread to the four of the guards burning them into trees. She then made the last one hang as she took his gun and shot him in the legs. 'So, who did you say wants me?' 'We don't know madam.' 'You don't know, really?' 'Yes, he just told us to get you to him now.' 'Lead the way.' they said, as she took him and walked to the place.

When she arrived, she killed the guy while he turned into a plant, the guards then came running as the plant grew bigger and bigger and then blasted green fire burning the guards and eating the rest of them. As more and more people, there was a guy with a cloak and a black-Grey mask that covered his eyes and hair. 'You must be Garies, how are you?' 'So it's you that's looking for me, huh?' 'Indeed, how are you?' 'Somewhat great, what do you want with me.' 'I need your help.' 'In what way?' 'The only way, come with me.' the guy said as he left, and she followed him.

When she got into this huge laboratory, there were a lot of people tracking different kinds of planets, even earth. 'What do you guys do?' 'Something-s, we need you to kill these kids.' 'Why is that.' 'They are highly risky to our universe, and you are the only one compatible to kill them all.' 'Well then, I can't wait.' Garies said, as she began to smile.

As the Dimensions landed on a new planet, it was so quiet. 'That's very suspicious.' 'Tell me about it.' 'So, I believe you know where the next portal is?' 'Yep, just two thousand mi-' before Ethan could finish, a thousand Wolves came running after the Dimensions as Wolves bit Thomas on his leg. 'Ahhh, they bit my leg, I need my leg.' '□□□□□□□□□□□ □□□□-' as Ethan tried to finish his sentence, again, a huge amount of fire that was green went all over Ethan burning him. 'Ethan, no!' Aries yelled.

As Ethan stopped burning, someone came out of nowhere with a dark cloak and started choking him. As Aries was about to attack him, the man then hit Ethan's chest as Ethan himself in spirit form, left his body. Clementine, Scott and Aries stood there with their mouths open as the man collected Ethan's spirit. As Aries tried to blast him, he then disappeared in a puff of smoke.

Clementine was then hit as she flew and hit the trees. The girl then burned Clementine with her green fire flames and Aries then grabbed her by her neck and before she could twist it, the girl grabbed Aries and threw her against Clementine, and in a fit of rage almost burned the both of them as Scott created a shield out of roots.

The girl then began to scream as the roots caught fire. Aries stood up and blasted the girl with her powers as TEACS started flying as he turned into his medium body and started blasting at the girl. As TEACS was about to transform into his huge body, a wolf came running as it bit TEACS's wing and before it could eat him, Clementine made the whole area dark and Aries blasted a huge amount of fire at the both of them.

As Clementine took away the darkness, the girls were gone and so were the Wolves.

PREVIEW¡

THE MAN WHO TOOK ETHAN'S SPIRIT

THE GIRL WHO HAS GREEN FLAMES

THE GIRL WHO WAS WITH THE WOLVES

'What just happened?' 'I don't know.' 'Uh, guys look at Thomas.' Scott said worriedly. As Aries and Clementine arrived, Thomas's legs began to turn hairy. 'Oh my Gosh, this is bad.' 'Whoever those guys were, they did something to you bad and they took Ethan's spirit.' 'Oh poor, TEACS, he's hurt.' 'I first need to find out who those people were?' 'Whoever they were, we have to find them, lord knows what they are going to do Ethan.' Clementine said.

As the guy who has Ethan's spirit, the girl with green flames and the girl with Wolves arrived at a huge cave, there was a lady who sat in the shadows.' So, did you get his spirit?''Yes ma'am, and his body.' 'Perfect, bring it here.' 'One thing, when am I getting my money.' 'You're pissing off, Angela.' 'Hell no, I want my money.' 'You want your money huh?, I'll give it to you.' said the lady as she absorbed Angela's green flames into her body. When she was done, Angela died as she turned into dust. 'Anyone of you that tries to piss me off, will get their powers taken away.' 'Yes, ma'am.' said the man.

As Aries, Clementine, Thomas And Scott were trying to find out where they has taken Ethan, more Wolves including lions and other animals that were green came in front of them. 'You have got to be kidding me.' 'Stay back, I've had enough of this.' Aries said as she blasted so hard that her fire got caught on the trees.

When she stopped, nothing happened to the animals as they came running to the four of the Dimensions. Before the wolves could bite Scott, Thomas turned into a wolf as he ran to the wolf and bit its head off. He then went for the lion as he clawed its eye and then bit the head off. As Thomas could howl, three arrows with green flames came flying and they hit Thomas, leaving him to lose consciousness.

Out of nowhere, a lady came with more of the green wolf, lion and other animals.

PREVIEW¡

'What the hell?' 'Well, Well, Well, if it isn't Aries?' 'How do the fuck do you know me?' 'Well, you are of course the one who has to be killed alongside your friends.' 'What are you talking about.' 'Taking your friend was the first step, she is going to take all of your powers.' 'Who is she?' 'Garies.' 'Do you know where she is?' Asked Clementine. 'Yes, that's cave over there.' 'Thanks, let's go.' Aries said.

When they arrived, Aries saw Ethan as Thomas ran to Scott and almost bit him as Clementine's new power came in and she looked in his eyes as Thomas started to back up. 'What's up with Thomas.' 'I did it.' Said the girl as more wolves came along. 'Who are you?' 'I'm Wolfina, I control Wolves.' 'And I'm spiriter.' said the man that took Ethan's soul. 'And I'm Garies.' said the lady in shadows as she stood up.

PREVIEW¡

'Just leave us alone.' 'I'm afraid I can't do that.' 'Then we have no choice, with the power we have left, let's save Ethan.' Aries said to the Dimensions. As Aries charged at Garies, Spiriter ran to Clementine to take her soul and before he could, she gave him a stare as he began to choke. Clementine then made his eyes dark and with a fist of rage, she hit him so hard that he hit a hole in the ground. Without him looking, she then killed him as she jumped on him.

Aries then ran up to Garies, Wolfina sent a herd of Wolves as they charged at Aries almost biting her as TEACS flew in and burned them all. More and More wolves chase Aries and TEACS let it all go and he blasted the huge fire, burning all the Wolves and Wolfina. Aries then hit Garies, as Garies's pet grew big and roared so loud that Aries went flying and hit the wall.

TEACS then ran and transformed into his huge form as she chased Garies's pet. Aries held a fist as she hit the ground and fire headed straight for Gaires, leaving for her to hit the top of the cave to the bottom. Aries then jumped on Garies with a fist of fire as Garies held it and twisted it. Garies then punched her and slapped her as she held her legs and threw her across the room. Garies then jumped punching Clementine and then hit her head against Clementine as she threw clementine and hit Scott. She then sat them in a cage and tied them up.

Aries was too weak, and Garies laughed in her dismay. As Garies took them, Aries lost it. As Aires got more angry and angry, TEACS then was absorbed into her as a mark of him appeared on her chest and a reflection of him made with fire at the back of her, and she blasted fire from her chest aiming at Garies as Garies and her pet burnt away in the dust.

PREVIEW!

The Dimensions stood in shook as Ethan's spirit went back into his body and Aires and TEACS split. 'That was amazing.' 'Thanks, I didn't want her hurt your guys.' 'I'm proud of you.' 'Thanks, hey! I see the portal.' 'What are we waiting for.' said Ethan as they tried to go through but the portal threw them back as it formed into five portals. 'What the?' Ethan said. 'Is that supposed to happen?' 'I don't think so.' 'What are we going to do.' 'There's only one way.' Ethan said.

CHAPTER 9

'The only way for us is to go through each portal.' 'So are you saying we have to split up?' 'Yes, that way we can tell each other which of us found the right portal.' 'Are you sure Ethan, we don't know what lies in these Portals?' 'Neither do I, but it will take longer if we through one by one.' 'I'm in.' said Aries. 'I'm in too.' said Scott. 'Me too.' said Thomas. It was just Clementine left as the rest of the Dimensions left. 'See you on the other side.' said Ethan as he jumped.And soon so did Clementine.

While Thomas was walking, he'd seen himself in a big wide forest. He then speeded around hoping to find a way out just as he bumped into someone. 'I'm sorry.' 'What are you doing here?' 'I'm investigating.' 'You need to leave.' 'Why.' 'YOU NEED TO LEAVE!' Yelled the person as they ran away. Thomas began to panic as the forest had a weird sound waving around him.

When he looked up, he saw the tallest creature as it looked at him with hunger.

PREVIEW:

Thomas ran for his life as the creature flew and hit his head. When he looked up, the creature used his tail to grab him as it flew away.

As Ethan jumped onto land, he saw weird creatures running away from the other direction. While he walked, someone bumped into him. 'It's almost here.' 'What's almost here?' 'It.' The guy said as he ran.

As Ethan turned around, he saw a huge creature looking at him as it blew so hard Ethan went flying across the deserted land.

PREVIEW;

'Who are you, foul peasant?' 'I'm Ethan and I am not a peasant.' 'Well then, I ll have you for dinner.' 'Over my dead body.' 'That can be arranged.' Said the godlike creature as Ethan ran so fast he tripped and fell. While falling, he saw a weird creature look at him as he hopped onto it and he rode off to who knows where....When Aries landed in wet mud, she suddenly stood in shock as she saw her reflection. 'We love Ethan but he will never love us, we are pathetic.' 'Who are you?' 'I'm you, son of a bitch.' 'Oh gosh, I'm dreaming aren't I, I knew this day would come, yeah, I should just wake up.' Said Aries.All of a sudden, her reflection screamed as Aries went flying across the mud. 'What the hell?' 'Don't you see, I'm you, actually, I'm a better you.' 'I'm fucked up.' Said Aries.

...Meanwhile, Clementine was sitting down as she waited for everyone to come. 'This sucks.' She sighed....As Thomas opened his eyes, he saw a billion creatures headed his way and he panicked. 'I told you guys I'd find the wizard.' 'Now we can get anything we want.' 'Um hello?' 'Ah, it speaks.' 'Of course, I speak, weirdos.' 'Do you do magic, my great wizard?' 'I'm not a wizard, and I will never be.'

'Well, that's, disappointing.' 'Well then, let's eat him.' 'Indeed!' The creature said as Thomas gulped.

Before they could grab Thomas, he jumped off the tangled rope and beat up as many creatures as he could but there were too many, so he did the only thing he could do. He quickly ran into a circle forming a tornado that had lightning striking in it. When the creatures went in it, they were all shocked that they turned into dust while Thomas made a run for it.

When he got outside, there were more creatures than there were in the room.

...Aries and her replica fought back-to-back until Aires started bleeding from her nose and mouth. 'I told you, I'm better than you.' 'No, this can't be happening.' 'Oh I'm sorry, but it is.' Said her replica, as Aries summoned TEACS and they combined as she blasted her replica into dust. 'I've never hated myself this much.' Cried, Aries.

Before she knew it, all the replicas appeared into a billion of them. 'What have I done wrong?' Cried Aries, as TEACS was shot and got injured. Soon all the replicas appeared in front of her as they all said, 'We are your biggest enemy!' and Aries screamed.

Ethan then stopped as he looked the godlike creature in the eye. 'What do you want from me?' 'Not you, but your powers and your friend's powers.' 'What?' 'Indeed, Don't you know it's me, the reason why all your friends are suffering, I took their fears and brought them to life.' 'What?' 'And I had to see you, otherwise you would've helped them as destroyed them.' 'And still am now.' Said Ethan as he activated his powers.

Soon Ethan blasted his beam as the godlike creature threw a little light ball that destroyed a hundred meters of land. 'Give it up Ethan, there's no hope for you destroying me.' 'Think again.' Said

Ethan, as he flew to the godlike creature and blasted him as the creature caught the blast and in a flash, the godlike creature's hand exploded. Ethan then ran and scream as he held the beam sword and cut open the throat of the godlike creature, whilst the blood poured over him.

Ethan then held the necklace the godlike creature was wearing and destroyed it.

All of a sudden, Thomas, Aries, Clementine, and Scott appeared where Ethan was and all five portals disappeared and turned into one as a new one appeared.

'I feel sick,' said Clementine as she threw up on Thomas. 'It could've been worse,' Thomas said.

As they entered the new portal, the dimensions were shot And Ethan was taken away from the rest of the dimensions, whilst they went underground.

CHAPTER 10

As the rest of the Dimensions were thrown into the cage, Ethan was taken to a castle where they hanged him, on a wall with huge pins on his hands.

As the rest of the Dimensions woke up, they felt drunk. 'Wha... Where am I?' 'Ah, you're awake.' 'Who are you?' 'There's no need for an introduction, you need to come with us.' 'No, who are you and where are we?' 'You are in the Kingdom of Tadum, where the great King Marlis lives.' said the man.

Soon one man and another were speaking to each other as they threw food into the dimensions. Scott and Thomas held hands as they fed each other, leaving Clementine to get jealous.

'What are we going to do guys?' 'I don't know, we have only one hour left with our powers, we need Ethan to activate them.' said Aries.

'It's going to be okay, Scott, we'll make it out alive.' 'Thomas, I have something to tell you, I've tried to tell you countless times.' 'What is it?' 'I... I... I love you.' said Scott as Thomas froze. 'Are you okay?' Asked Scott. Thomas just stood up and went to the corner as Scott felt hurt.

Hours and hours passed by as Scott and Thomas hadn't spoken to each other and they haven't eaten. 'Please sir, we're hungry.' 'Shut the hell up, we all have lives here.' said the man.

Clementine got upset, and with the anger boiling, she screamed as the bar bent open and the man split in half. She then turned her head anticlockwise as her eyes turned fully black and the wall broke down. Woah, that was amazing.' 'Let's go save Ethan.

As Ethan was being hanged, fifteen soldiers with silver pants walked up to Ethan as a tall white man with a crown walked in between the soldiers.

'Ethan Reddy, what a pleasure to finally meet you.' 'Wh... Where am I?' said Ethan as they beat him with a wooden stick. 'You're in the great Kingdom Tadum, and I've been searching for you Ethan, for the past nine chapters.' 'What are you talking about?' 'Your powers Ethan, are greater than any powers I've ever seen.' 'Then why did you kidnap me?' 'Why, because I want those powers, I need those powers, so I created a portal that would you bring you to me and it worked.' 'You... Are sick.' 'I'm not, I'm just getting what I want.' 'Yeah, you're not sick, you're a spoilt brat.' 'It doesn't matter what you say, the commencement of taking your powers will take place tomorrow, I'll rule the universe with your powers.' Laughed King Tadum.

As the rest of the Dimensions were walking, Scott and Thomas looked at each other with fear and love. 'We're here.' 'Oh, cool.' 'But this is just a cave.' 'That's right, it's where we are going to sleep.' 'Uhm, okay.' Said Clementine.

As they lay down, Thomas jumped up and screamed, as a purple crystal almost hit him. 'Where did this come from?' Asked Clementine. 'From me.' said the man.

Soon a teenage boy walked in as he looked at the dimensions with a grin on his face. 'Who are you?' 'Christal, possessor of the purple crystals and I've been sent to kill you by King Tadum.' 'Why does the king wanna kill us?' 'Simple, he knows you want to get Ethan, while he wants Ethan's powers.' 'Well, I'm sorry, we will destroy you.' said Aries as Clementine pulled in. 'Are you crazy, once we use our powers, they disappear and we'll need Ethan, who is not here, to reactivate them?' 'Well, that's not going to stop me from killing this guy.' 'Dimensions, let's do this.' said Aries.

Aries then jumped and blasted a huge ball of fire at Christal as the blocked it with a shield of his crystals. He then started forming crystals in his hand as he prepared to aim them at Aires.

PREVIEW:

After blasting them at Aires, Aries went flying across the room with the crystal in her arm. 'Ah!' yelled Aries. Scott then made tree monsters as they grabbed Christal by his legs and swung him to the other trees. Christal then punched the ground as a thousand crystals blasted from the soil, ripping the tress bit by bit, that too hitting Scott in his hand.

As Thomas tried to create an electric tornado, Christal blasted his crystals right into Thomas's foot and ear. It was only Clementine and Christal left as Aries yelled, 'Scream Clementine, SCREAM!' but Clementine knew she couldn't do it for she could lose her powers.

'Give it up cutie, there's no hope left.' said Christal as he formed the hugest crystal, ready to aim at Clementine. Clementine then had an idea as she looked Christal in the eye while he threw the crystal. Too afraid to watch, the rest of the dimensions closed their eyes. As Clementine caught the crystal, a huge blast destroyed the mountain. As Christal looked, he was shocked to see Clementine had caught the crystal. 'I... Impossible.' said Christal, as Clementine threw it back to him, not only killing him but causing a huge explosion.

The Dimensions then stood up and continued the journey to find Ethan with what just happened.

As Ethan was being pulled, he had a vision of seeing the dimensions getting injured and Clementine killing Christal. He then knew that they needed to reactivate their powers. So with all the breath and strength he had, Ethan then said, 'DIMENSIONS... ASSEMBLE!' as the dimensions stopped and their powers activated, leaving their eyes to glow their colours.

'Ethan did it, he did it.' 'What are we waiting for, let's save him.' Said Aries.

They then sat him on a long rectangular bed while connecting wires to his arms, legs, and head. 'I can't believe this is happening, I will finally be the king I'm meant to be.' said King Tadum.

The bed then rotated left as it went straight, and the wires started to glow. Before his powers could be absorbed, Clementine screamed so loud that the building shook and all the machinery and wires split open.

'What the, who are they?' 'It's over king Tadum, give us Ethan and we'll be out of your way.' 'I'm afraid I can not do that, Ethan's powers are mine, I've searched too long to give it up, Waterna, take these punks out.' said King Tadum as water flow through the room, and then formed into a girl.

PREVIEW;

'I strongly suggest you get out of here.' 'No can do.' said Clementine, as she screamed but Waterna just turned into water and back. 'You stupid girl.' Waterna said as she sent water swords flying to them when one actually cut Thomas's thumb off.

Before they knew it, Christal, Wolfina, and the Speedos came jumping out of Portals and ran straight to them. 'Oh my gosh, Scott cover us.' said Clementine as Scott created a shield with roots.

'Oh my gosh, what are we going to do?' 'I don't know, I wish Ethan were here.' 'We have to do something, they're going to kill him.' 'You're right, come on Clementine, you come up with the best plans.' said Aries.

Clementine then looked around as she looked at the dimensions and came up with a plan. 'I'm going to scream, sending them away, while Aries fights Wolfina, Scott fights Christal, Thomas will create a tornado, absorbing the speedos and I'll take care of Waterna.' 'That's actually a good idea.' 'Are you ready guys?' 'Yeah.' Said Aries as Scott removed the shield and Clementine screamed, blowing away the speedos and Christal's crystals and Wolfinas Wolves.

Aries then jumped, forming a huge fireball that destroyed half of the castle and Wolfinas wolves, but she was able to generate more from her hand. 'This will be fun.' said Aries as she called TEACS and he came in his second form, taking out the wolves while Aries kept on blasting Wolfina.

Scott then created poison ivy plants sending them to Christal as he created a crystal shield and blasted thousands of Crystal, destroying the poison ivy plants, but without noticing, one of the plants touched his face, causing a big itch, while Scott sent a sharp stick into Christal's heart, while he broke down in crystals.

Thomas felt weak, he couldn't even move a muscle, and all the speedos came running towards him. Before they could touch him, Scott created a huge root that caught all of them. 'Thomas, you can do this, you can do that tornado, you got this.' 'But I'm injured.' 'Just try, you'll never know unless you try.' Said Scott as Thomas stood up and began to run in a circular motion.

Soon the speedos went in the tornado as Scott began to cover it with roots. Aries saw what was happening as she made Wolfina and her wolves fly to Thomas's tornado, by transforming with TEACS, using her wings to blow them away. When all of them were in the Tornado, Scott covered it up with the roots and Aries blasted the fire flames into the roots, burning all the wolves and speedos.

It came down to Clementine and Waterna, as Waterna thought that she will able to capture Clementine into a waterball, but clementine just made her eye black as she hypnotized Waterna and made herself freeze and Aries blasted her into ashes.

Aries, Clementine, Scott, And Thomas stood as they looked at King Tadum. 'Well... Well, you kids are really exceptional, you destroyed all of those creatures, Wow.' 'It's over King Tadum, hand over Ethan.' 'it's not over until I say it's over.' said king Tadum as more Portals opened up and all the same people came flying back into the castle, multiplied. 'Holy guacamoly.' said Aries. 'What are we going to do now, it's impossible for the tornado to absorb them all.' said Thomas. Clementine knew the only person who could kill them all and stop the portals from opening, was Ethan. 'We have to get Ethan, he's the only one who can destroy them.' said Clementine.

Clementine then went to Thomas and she said, 'I need you to take me to Ethan, while Aries and Scott try to distract King Tadum.' said Clementine as Thomas nodded.

Scott then made all the creature slide to King Tadum as Aries blasted all the soldiers. When Clementine made it to Ethan, Thomas was bitten by a wolf and his inner wolf took over him.'T homas, no?' yelled Clementine as she screamed and he flew away.

'Ethan, we need you, we need you Ethan.' said Clementine but Ethan didn't wake up. She kept repeating her words but he still didn't wake up. It was then when Clementine cupped Ethan's face with her hands as she kissed him and the power of darkness and the power of lightness merged together, causing a huge explosion to destroy not only the castle but the whole of Tadum. 'No!' yelled King Tadum as all the creatures died and the portals closed.

Everyone was on the ground as Ethan woke up and ran to Aries to check if she was okay, and Clementine was hurt. King Tadum then saw Ethan and before he could absorb his powers, he saw Clementine and all the anger, fear, and love mixed with her powers. He then knew that she was the source he'd been looking for.

Without hesitation, he ran and jumped into Clementine as they merged, forming a tall and powerful king Tadine, and a white wolf. 'No, Clementine.' Yelled Ethan.

'I was stupid, Clementine carries more power than you, Ethan.' 'Let her go, Tadum.' 'No can do, I've searched too long to let this precious power go,' said King Tadum, as he blew from his mouth causing the dimensions to fly across. Ethan quickly stood up and jumped as he bean-blasted Tadine and he fell breaking Kingdom Tadum into half. Ethan then blasted a beam at Tadine as they used clementines powers and hypnotized Ethan. Before Ethan was about to beam himself, he broke the hypnotize and destroyed the whole planet.

Right now, there was nothing left of Tadum, and Everyone except the dimensions, was killed. As Ethan and Tadine met eye to eye, Tadine held a fist as he said, 'This ends now.' and he let go of a huge portal that started to absorb everything.

PREVIEW;

As the dimensions tried to hold on, Thomas, Scott, and Aries were absorbed leaving Ethan levitating. 'Clementine is mine.' 'No, she isn't.' said Ethan as he flew to Tadine, but before he could attack, the portal increased the absorption and sucked Ethan.

SOME OTHER PLANET...

The Dimensions fell from the sky in a mud puddle. 'Clementine.' 'She's gone, forever.' 'No, she isn't.' 'Ethan, you saw what happened to her, we'll just have to continue the journey without her.' said Aries, as the dimensions continued walking to the next portal.

Out of nowhere, Ethan stopped as his eyes turned white and he saw Clementine, in his arms, weak and pale while king Tadum yelled,'NO!'

'Stop,' yelled Ethan. 'What, what is it?' 'We have to go get Clementine.' 'Ethan, did you not-' 'No, I had a vision, I saw Clementine, we have to save her.' 'But how sure are we?' 'It seems the Portals are changing direction... To kingdom Tadum,' said Thomas. 'You see, we have to save her.' 'Fine then, let's do it.' said Aries, as the dimensions continued their journey.

While Thomas and Scott were walking, Scott held Thomas by his waist and smelt his neck. 'Stop.' 'I don't care if you don't love me, I love you.' 'Scott, stop.' 'Fine, but I'll be waiting for you, no matter how long it takes,' said Scott, as Thomas looked away and held his hand tight, which led to the both of them blushing.

Meanwhile...

'Now that I have gotten rid of Ethan, I will finally create my universe, no, GALAXY!, Let's begin.' said Tadine as he blasted black smoke a human being appeared, and he then chuckled.

CHAPTER 11

As they kept walking, Thomas and Scott couldn't stop holding hands, they just wanted to kiss and cuddle as everything around them disappeared but Thomas was still unsure of his feelings as he looked at Scott and turned peach red. Both gazing into each other's eye, there was a voice that said, 'Nothing is better than love,' and the Dimensions turned around, eyeing a huge creature that was exactly like a heart.

'What in the mother of love,' Ethan said as the creature moved closer to them, smiling. 'I'm Loverz, the love lady and you guys in the worlc of Love!' she exclaimed. Soon people entered the premises as they cheered in joy for the Dimensions. 'We love you.' 'I love you.' 'They love you very much.' 'It's just Us that love you so much,' they all said, terrifying the Dimensions.

'Here at Loverz wolrd, Love lives, no sadness, hate or anger, just love,' she said when a rainbow appeared in front of her. 'Wow,' Aries said. The Dimensions were then escorted to a palace, where people were dancing and singing in joy when Scott and Thomas immediately ran to the food stall.

As Tadine was walking around, he kept on thinking about how was he going to create his universe, his galaxy, his Dimension. He then sat down and came up with a plan. He knew that if there were multiple universes, galaxies and dimensions, there had to be one that had a person who had the power of creation. Tadine then closed his eyes as a million black spirits whispering names surrounded his mind. Finally, he found the perfect one he could use as he blasted black energy and it formed a portal into which he entered, heading for the specific person.

Everyone was having a wonderful time as others kissed and others kept dancing. Despite figuring it out, Thomas went to Scott, grabbed his hand and danced with him. Thomas held Scott's hands as they danced, moving their body around and around when Thomas gripped his hand in Scott's waist and twisted him, leaving Scott to fall in his arms. They then stood still as Thomas wrapped his hands around Scott's body and laid his head on Scott's head. They both fell hot and felt their stomachs fill with butterflies. Thomas then turned him around, both of them facing each other. Eye to eye. Lip to lip. Body to body.

As Thomas leaned closer, they immediately parted ways as Loverz interrupted their scene. 'Aren't you guys so in love,' she said, making the both of them blush.

Upon seeing this, Ethan left the room being followed by Aries. They both sat down, watching the stars when Ethan burst into tears. Aries didn't want to but she let him lay his head on her shoulder. 'Talk to me,' she said. 'I... I... I miss her, I just want her to be here, with us, right now,' Ethan said as he sat upright. 'But you had a vision that you saved her, don't worry, you'll get her.' 'Will I? It's just a vision, the future isn't set in stone, plus I had her in my arms pale and weak, I... I... Let her down, I let everybody down,' Ethan said, falling to his knees.

'Don't say that, you are the most bravest and responsible leader I've ever met, for what it's worth, you're the only reason why we're still standing, it's all thanks to you,' Aries said, glaring into Ethan's eyes. Ethan stood up and hugged her when Aries gasped.

During the hug, Ethan saw a house that kept moving. He then left Aries and walked over there. Both of them were scared but the house kept on shaking harder and harder and worse when they heard voices. Holding each other's hands, Aries blasted the door open, finding themselves facing people who were so pale.

They entered, seeing people who were crying in corners, yelling at how much they hated life and worst of all, people who had committed suicide by hanging themselves. They were shocked.

When King Tadine landed on the floor, the area was quiet. As he took three steps, he was intruded on by five men with chains installed in their hands that were connected to knives.

'Who here knows where I can find Poean?' he asked but no response. Before he could speak, one of them threw the knives at him but King Tadine grabbed the knife, which cut him, and pulled the guy towards him, punching him to the floor and stabbing the knife in his chest.

'If it's a fight you want, it's a fight you'll get,' Tadine said as the rest of the men charged at him. They started swaying the knives around as the other cut Tadine's finger off. Holding in the pain, Tadine jumped to him and twisted his neck, cutting his hand off and using the guy's chain to kill the others. He stabbed the others not noticing that the other ones came from behind and tried cutting his head off when Tadine grabbed the knife and swung the man around. Finally stopping him, Tadine wrapped the guy's chain around his neck and choked the guy to death.

Wiping the blood of him, ten new men entered but with a man that was as tall as Tadine. 'This is gonna be fun.' 'I see you seek the name, Poean, come with me,' said the itinerant person as Tadine followed him.

They then sat down, when the unknown person showed him a picture and said, 'This is Poean, unfortunately for you, she is locked up, in a different galaxy, because she created things that should not have been created and almost ended all life as we know it,' said the stranger as he opened his drawer and searched for something. He then placed a card on the table and said to Tadine, 'This person in this universe, knows where Poean is, I must warn you, he is dangerous.' the man said as Tadine took the card but was stopped by the same men.

Without time to spare, Tadine let the black smoke out which went into the men's mouths and killed them all, including the itinerant person.

Tadine then laughed, entering the portal to the next victim.

Ethan kept on asking why the people were behaving like this but they were too full of hating life. 'What are we going to do?' asked Aries. Luckily Ethan stood still and his eyes turned white.

He then saw Loverz lifting Thomas and Scott in the air as she was absorbing their love for each other. When he got back to reality, ignoring Aries's question, Ethan took her and ran back to the Palace.

They were faced with the same situation as Aries blasted fire at Loverz with separated her from Thomas and Scott. 'So this is what you do, make people fall in love and take it later,' Ethan said in anger. 'No, I make people fall in love and take it but I was shocked upon seeing the love Thomas and Scott have for each other, especially you and Aries,' she said as the Dimensions stood next to each other. When Ethan said, 'DIMENSIONS ASSEMBLE!' Their powers awoke and Loverz charged at them.

Before the Dimensions could attack, Loverz had already started sucking their love. Losing their feelings and emotions, the Dimensions were helpless but when Ethan looked outside, he remembered that the only thing that can stop love is hate.

With the energy he had left, Ethan beam-blasted Loverz as he made a run for it. When he arrived at the house, he yelled, 'DON'T YOU WANT THE WHOLE PLANET TO FEEL HATE, SADNESS AND WORST OF DEPRESSION, COME OUT AND SPREAD IT!' Ethan yelled as the people ran out of the house, to the palace.

They all jumped on Loverz as she tried to take their love, but they didn't have any. When she was stuck and couldn't move, Ethan ran and jumped, forming his sword and stabbing Loverz as she began to convulse.

'She's going to blow,' said Thomas. The Dimensions quickly grabbed the food and sprinted as fast as they could when finally, Loverz exploded, killing all the citizens of Loverz world and when the Dimensions jumped in the portal, the whole planet burst from the inside.

SOMEWHERE IN THE GALAXY...

She walked over to her throne, sitting aside three other men. A man came running in with a paper, leaving for the women to smile. 'What is it you have for me?' 'It's her, they found her,' he said showing her the picture. 'Perfect, She's Perfect,' the woman said, grinning.

CHAPTER 12

As he landed on the grass, he found himself looking at an open land. In the middle of the land, there was a bar that had loud music and stomping from there. Tadine then made his way to the bar as he saw another house but small and about ten meters from where he was.

He made his way in as everyone looked at him. The whole bar was filled with drunkard men. As he went over to the bartender, he asked for a glass of water with a bit of milk. When he drank the liquid, all the gentlemen looked at him. They started to laugh as everything went into a blur.

Tadine then tried to walk but two men grabbed his hands and tied them together. In his weak state, Tadine fell to his knees and blacked out.

He opened his eyes and saw the men surrounding him as the other grabbed chains and started swaying them around. Tadine got furious as he commanded that they set him free. The guy then hit Tadine as he screamed in pain. He then hit him with the other chain which grabbed his flesh and pulled it off him.

Tadine got mad when he saw blood drop from his back. When the guy whipped the chain again, Tadine grabbed it and pulled the guy towards him, placing the chains around his neck and cutting him open.

The rest of the men then grabbed swords, guns, knives more chains as they faced Tadine but he grinned, activating his power.

When the Dimensions arrived at the new planet, it too was open land. No houses. No trees. No water. Just mud and sand. 'Any luck finding the next portal?' Asked Aries. 'Nope,' Ethan replied.

They walked eight kilometres and no portal was seen. Ethan then fell to his knees as Aries rushed over to him. 'The portal is nowhere close and we're wasting time to get to Clementine, I should have never let her save me, now I regret it,' Ethan said.

Out of nowhere, he was dragged into the air as his eyes turned black and his hands with his legs facing behind him. Aries, Scott and Thomas yelled out for Ethan but he was stuck in the trans.

Aries then tells Scott to send Roots to bring him down but he's unsuccessful without Ethan's commands, their powers fade away. Aries then also starts to feel regret as she falls to her knees and is also ascended into the air, her eyes turning black and her arms and legs facing behind her. Scott tried his best to command his powers but they were gone as he felt weak. Thomas then looked up and said, 'I should've helped Ethan, we're a team and I'm just letting him feel this way plus I'm hiding my love from you. I'm stupid. I'm nothing. I'm useless,' as also escalated into the air, eyes turned to black and his legs with arms behind him not long when Scott also felt regret for not telling Thomas that everything he said was false, and into the air he went as well.

They all were under the spell as their regrets were being absorbed by something.

Tadine then used the same chain and swung it around one of the men's necks, using them to hit the others. As the others threw knives, he quickly dodged them and made them hit the men with swords. Tadine swang the chain to the roof as he used it to jump up and sent Clemetine's powers to force them to kill others. Murder, screams and blood was made as Tadine laughed, sitting on the ceiling.

After ten minutes, he reversed the powers and jumped, eyeing the last guys left. 'I didn't come here to fight or play, I came here for Cithadel,' he said as the man's facial expressions went to shock. 'You don't know, do you?' 'Know what?' asked Tadine as he sat down.

'I'm sure you saw the house across our bar. That's where Cithadel lives since her sister was arrested.' the man said. 'Why was she arrested?' Tadine asked. 'She wanted to create her own universe where she and her sister could live, with peace and freedom. But then the space army won't fond of her plan as it could kill other lives and maybe end humanity as we know it. So her sister was arrested and Cithadel didn't take it well. She nearly killed all our men. After the attack, she ran towards that house and lived there, never came out,' the man said, grabbing his wine and drinking it.

Tadine then looked through the window and saw Cithadel's house. He knew he had to get to her sister no matter what. So he grabbed his stuff and made his way over to her building.

The Dimensions then opened their eyes as the person they had Regret for appeared in front of them. As Ethan looked at Clementine, she slapped him and cried. 'Why didn't you save me?

We're a team. You're our leader. But no, you left me there. You let me die. You let Tadum take me so he can use my powers. That's right, it's all your fault,' she said as Ethan fells to his knees and cried louder than before. Aries saw Ethan as he walked over to her and said,'If you really loved me, you would've helped me by now. You would've helped me find Clementine. But you didn't. You don't love me. You don't care about me. You'd rather let me commit suicide and die,' and Aries too fell to her knees, crying tearfully.

It was different when Thomas and Scott had both each other say Negative things but the love these two had for each other was too powerful as Scott said,'I know Thomas would never say those words to me. He said it himself, he loves me!' and the whole vision started to crack as it exploded and Scott fell, seeing his friends up in the air. Scott then screamed out Thomas's name as he fell and landed on Scott. They did the same to Aries but were unsuccessful when Ethan looked at them and beam blasted them, sending them flying. 'Ethan please, you can fight it,' Aries said but the possession of Ethan was too powerful.

The ground then started to convulse as a huge misty creature burst from it and eyed the Dimensions. 'What are you?' Thomas said. 'I'm REGRET, the one controlling your friend,' the creature said, forcing Ethan to send lights towards the Dimensions and then blasting all of them, leaving them weak on the ground.

Tadine then blasted the door down as a girl came out and screamed. The scream was her power, as she sent Tadine's flesh peeling off. Tadine then clapped which sent a wave, forcing her to fall to the ground. He then made his levitate as he forced her to tell him where her sister was. 'She's in prison, dumbass,' said Cithadel as Tadine forced her to tell him how he could get her.

'I'm not going to tell you. You don't understand what it means to be hated because you want something,' Cithadel said as Tadine released her and said, 'I do know. That's why I want your sister to create my galaxy. I've been shamed. Hunted and almost killed. I want to control people. I want people who will worship me. That's why I want your sister,' Tadine said as Cithadel looked at him, suspiciously.

'How can I trust you?' Cithadel asked. 'I know the story those men told me was a lie and now you can get your revenge by killing them. They're coming right now to try to kill us both,' Tadine said as the men arrived.

The men then started throwing armour and weapons as Cithadel took a deep breath in and screamed so loud, not only their skin came off but as well as their bones. They were turned into dust as Tadine laughed.

He then opened a portal as Cithadel went through and Tadine laughed, heading for the next location.

Aries went flying as she pulled Thomas with her. Scott then ran as roots picked him up and dragged him all the way to Ethan. Ethan then used the sword he formed and cut the root, leaving Scott to fall and he then blasted Scott, injuring his hand. Aries tried to form a fireball but Ethan just jumped towards her and punched her. He then grabbed her and smashed her against the ground.

Ethan was holding Aries in the air while his hands were wrapped around her neck. Aries then said, 'Ethan please, you have to resist. Just think about what will happen when you save Clementine. You... You saw it. Y-You saw Her. Come... Come on,' she said as she was close to letting out her last breath.

Ethan remembered the vision and dropped Aries as he screamed and the whole planet exploded. Regret then tried to stop Ethan as he sent whispers of regret heading for his ears. Ethan then beam-blasted regret as it exploded and died.

Ethan hugged Aries as she blushed. 'Thanks. I don't know what I'd do without you,' Ethan said, smiling at Aries. When they saw the next portal, Ethan's eyes then turned white as he arrived on a different planet.

He saw a man and girl, destroying a planet, killing millions of lives. The man then said,'Have you seen her sister?' but the person didn't respond as the girl screamed and killed a quarter of people. When Ethan looked into the man's eyes, he saw Clementine. He saw the girl he had been searching for. As he tried to stop them, he literally passed through them, remembering that this was all a vision.

His eyes turned back to their normal colour and Ethan started breathing heavily. 'What's wrong?' Aries asked. 'I... I saw him. I saw Tadum and he's going to destroy planets,' Ethan said, trying to catch his breath.

'Well, what are we going to do? The portal leads to another planet,' said Scott as they looked concerned. 'I don't know. We have to stop him. He's killing innocent people,' Ethan said, as a tear dropped from his eye.

They just stood there as a white light appeared. It was so bright, you couldn't look at it. When it burst, a hole appeared which was to a planet that had already been destroyed.'Woah,' Scott said. 'How?' Aries said. 'I don't know but this is our chance to stop Tadum and that girl,' Ethan said as he walked through the portal with the Dimensions.

Chapter 13

Tadine threw the three police officers to the wall as one of them broke his neck. 'Tell us how to get my sister back!' Cithadel demanded an answer. 'She's under the security of the most powerful guards there is. Not only is her powers locked, she is brutally beaten if she tries to use her powers let alone escape. I doubt she'd be alive,' the officer said as Cithadel began to tear up. She then looked at the guards and screamed, peeling not only their flesh but as well as their bones.

Cithadel then looked at the towns and cities and screamed so loud that the whole planet shook. Buildings started to fall as well as the ground cracked. Tadine then headed to the owner of the planet and he asked him where Cithadel's sister was but he said he had no clue, so Tadine looked him in the eye and his head exploded. As Tadine created another portal to another planet, the whole planet exploded, sending asteroids to other planets.

As the Dimensions land on a planet, they didn't break any bones. 'Where are we and why is the ground so soft!' Aries said, falling to the ground. 'I know right, it's amazing-' 'We don't have time to enjoy the ground, we have to stop Tadine before he destroys more planets and kills more people,' Ethan said, heading for the next portal.

'I still don't get why we must cross a whole planet to get to the other port-' Aries said as the planet began to convulse. Ethan immediately yelled "DIMENSIONS ASSEMBLE!" as they activated their abilities.

They heard a croaking noise around them but couldn't see where it was coming from. As they formed a protection circle, a long string of wool grabbed Scott's leg and dragged all the way to the top as Aries tried burning it. There it was, a wool creature that jumped on Aries, tying her up from her hands and legs. Ethan then cuts the wool as Thomas grabs Aries and takes to Scott as she blasts the wool and burns all the lead and wool on this planet.

The Dimensions then are faced with more of the wool creatures as Scott tries to smash them with a wood hammer but somehow he can't. 'What's wrong?' 'I don't know, it's like my powers faded,' Scott said as one of the creatures jumped in and the lead took him. Aries tried to blast as well but couldn't as her powers too disappeared and got dragged by lead.

Ethan and Thomas tried to run but couldn't as the creatures used the lead to catch up to them and took them as well.

They were on their knees, begging for mercy but Cithadel was too upset as she screamed and killed twenty innocent kids on the eleventh planet they had destroyed. Cithadel then falls to her knees as she has memories of her sister and wonders if she is dead. 'She's not, don't worry,' Tadine said. 'How sure are you, we've been destroying so many planets and I still have no answer, all we have to sector G137,' Cithadel said, continuing to cry.

Tadine then began to think hard about the letter and number Cithadel said that they got from the guard. He then remembered that he still had the card from where he was. He knew that Pena knew where Sector G137 was. Tadine picked up Cithadel and opened a portal, lucky enough to get to Pena.

'Finally, I was awaiting your arrival,' Pena said, turning around and facing Tadine and Cithadel. 'I want to know where Cithadel is?' he asked. 'That's where Poena is.' 'Yeah, no shit,' Tadine said. Pena then laughed as Tadine and Cithadel looked confused.

With Anger, Cithadel killed the two women around Pena, screaming. 'You don't know how many people I've killed, you don't know what I've done to get here. If you don't tell me where my sister is, I'm going to kill you, your loved ones and finally, past you. So please, tell me where the heck sector G137 is or so help me I'll-' 'Fine, it's by planet Girth, the main prison for all alien prisoners,' Pena said, shivering.

'Thank you for your service,' Cithadel said as Tadine opened the portal and they entered it.

Cithadel and Tadine laughed as they entered the new planet. 'I don't think this is Girth, so much wool and lead,' Cithadel said as lead grabbed both Tadine and Cithadel. Cithadel then screamed as all of the lead turned into dust and flew away.

The Dimensions then fell as they begged the people for food. While Tadine was examining the wool and lead, Cithadel gave them the food they had. The Dimensions stood up and thanked her as Ethan looked at the girl and beam blasted her. Cithadel when flying as Tadine caught her. 'What the heck?' 'Look, Aries,' Thomas said, eyeing Tadine and Cithadel together, who were in Ethan's visions.

'Well, Well, Well, look who it is,' Tadine said as Ethan didn't hesitate.

Ethan immediately formed his sword as he ran towards Tadine. Cithadel stood in front of Tadine as she began to scream. Before the scream could hit Ethan, Aries blasted her and Ethan slid on her knees, avoiding the scream. Ethans charged at Tadine as he grabbed the sword and tried to stab Ethan, forgetting that's it Ethan's power as Ethan blasted him, sending him to the ground.

Aries tried to blast Cithadel again but Cithadel was quick as she screamed and their fire and vocal were competing. As the scream of Cithadel was able to push Aries fire, Scott sent knife roots that flew to Cithadel, stabbing her in her leg. When she fell, Aries blasted her and sent Cithadel flying.

Weak on the ground, Ethan looked at Tadine and saw her. He saw Clementine, trapped in there. Tadine knew what was Ethan's weakness as he tricked him and used Clementine's voice.

'Why didn't you save me? Why didn't you stop him,' Tadine said, standing up. I'm sorry. I knew I should've but it's okay, I'm here.' 'Are you,' Tadine said as he looked Ethan in the eye and got control of him.

The Dimensions then saw Tadine possess Ethan as they tried to stop him but Cithadel screamed too loud she sent them hitting each other which lead to Scott breaking his arm and Thomas breaking his leg.

Tadine then prepared to extract Ethan's powers as the Dimensions, weak, screamed Ethan's name so he could wake up but the possession was too strong. Ethan then ascended as his powers were leaving him and entering Tadine.

As the powers were halfway into Tadine, the ground started to convulse and out of nowhere, a huge hole opened, blasting hot lava onto Tadine, who was screaming in pain. Ethan then landed as a rope from the hole headed for Aries and tied her up. Ethan woke up and saw Tadine, weak on the ground, in Cithadel's arms as he knew he finally had the chance to end Tadum and get Clementine back but he then heard screams when he saw Aries being dragged into the fiery hole.

It was then that Ethan had to decide between Aries and Clementine. Ethan then ran to Aries as he tried to pull her back but the fire in the hole fought back, sending fire dogs that grabbed Ethan and started biting him. Ethan then formed his beam sword and started slicing the heads off the fire creatures.

Ethan then saw the fear in Aries's eyes as he tried his best to catch her but the hole took her and Ethan saw her fall in. Her legs and arms were swinging as Aries called out Ethan's name and as Ethan tried to jump in, the hole closed and exploded, destroying the whole planet.

Ethan coughed as he stood up and saw Tadine, who was entering a portal with Cithadel. He immediately blasted a beam of light at them but he didn't make it in time as the Portal closed and Tadine escaped.

Ethan couldn't believe it. Aries was taken away. Tadine, who had Clementine, escaped. And the portal was nowhere to be seen. As Scott and Thomas came to him, he hugged them and cried. They then let him lay on their laps as Ethan cried all the Love, Regret and Pain out.

When they arrived, Tadine and Cithadel were shocked to see the prison. After all that killing and murder, they finally made it to Sector G137.

CHAPTER 14

She held a ball of fire as she could feel the heat, tossing the burning flame to him as he fell. He stood up and caught the flame, sending it back to her with ten more. She then jumped as she transformed into fire flame heading towards him. The men then told her not to but she ignored them as she clashed with him and exploded.

She came falling just as she hit the ground, creating a hole. 'Flame Queen, are you okay?' 'I need you to take care of her, make sure she finds the right one because he is-' she said, coughing. '-coming back and he will end all fire element possessors,' she said as she kept on coughing just as she closed her eyes.

The man screamed as the other grabbed his arm and ran with the little girl in their arms.

THIRTEEN YEARS LATER

She commanded the chef to make the food more enjoyable because she had been waiting too long for the food. Just as she walked over to her throne, sitting aside three other men. A man came running in with a paper, leaving for the women to smile.

'What is it you have for me?' 'It's her, they found her,' he said showing her the picture. 'Perfect, She's Perfect,' the woman said, grinning.

'What are you waiting for? We must get it immediately no time to waste!' she said as the guards rang the bell of gathering.

MOMENTS LATER

They stood in a circle as the Princess made her way to the center. She took out the staff which held the ultimate power of fire. She raised it above her knees as all the fire on the planet ascended. When she dropped it, the fire receded, opening a portal.

They then saw a girl who tried to get out of the portal but Princess Fire hit the staff again and made the girl fall as the portal closed and the girl lost consciousness. 'It's her,' a woman said as Princess Fire gave one more look.

'Take her to the Castle. It's time!' Princess Fire said as the guards took Aries to the castle.

Tadine and Cithadel jumped in joy, eyeing the place that they have been waiting for, Sector G137, also known as, Polluck Prison.

As they took three steps further, immediately they were attacked by a thousand guards. With all the anger, Cithadel screamed so loud, she instantly killed half of the guards. As she closed her mouth, the other guards shot her, injuring her arm. Tadine immediately acted out as he started to whisper.

His eyes turned dark and black smoke left his hands as it entered the guards, whispers entering their ears and they fainted.

Tadine picked up Cithadel as he and she made their way to the prison. There were people screaming and others crying when Cithadel eyed her sister's cell, which was the largest cell and protected by this huge, strong and indestructible guard.

'NO ONE WILL PASS!' He said as his words were so loud it blew wind towards Tadine and Cithadel.

She woke up, breathing heavily as she saw two men standing in front of the door. Aries wondered where she was when a beautiful woman entered the room. Aries wanted to blast her but remembered Ethan wasn't near her for a long time.

'Who are you and why am I here?' she said, eyeing Princess Fire. 'I'm Princess Fire and you are the chosen one. You have to battle with Goaub. The Lord of fire,' Princess Fire said as she walked over to the window.

'I would love to fight but I have to help my friends save another friend, so please,' Aries said as she stood up and headed for the door.

Princess Fire blasted a fireball toward her, freezing her in the position she was in.

'You don't understand, Aries. You are the only fire possesser who can stop Goaub from taking all the fire abilities. You must fight!' exclaimed Princess Fire as she walked towards Aries.

She held Aries's hand when they both looked up and Aries saw a land full of dead people.

People were begging for mercy when Gouab absorbed their abilities and ended their lives. He then used the fire to destroy other planets and burn the people to their death.

Aries then saw a person behind him and was shocked to see herself, levitating with a flame around her.

She immediately came back to reality, breathing heavily. 'You see if you don't stop him, all life could end. Only you can stop him, Only you!' Princess Fire said when she let go of Aries's hand, letting out a stressful sigh.

As Aries tries to talk to Princess Fire, a huge fire hand came through the room, hitting Princess Fire on the door while Aries hid under the bed.

The hand then took Princess Fire as a fireball flew in, exploding the whole room.

Smoke was everywhere as Aries tried to look for a way out, she saw Princess Fire and a huge fire giant facing each other. She immediately knew that that was Goaub.

They let out a relieved yawn just as they saw Ethan eyeing the planet that had been destroyed. They stood up and made their way to him, holding each other's hands. Just as they touch his shoulders, Ethan's eyes turn white and he looks upwards, opening his mouth.

He then lands in a field full of fire. Ethan screams "Hello" but no answer as he hears a crash. He heads for the crash when he faced Aries, begging for help. He tries to help her but can't because it's a vision.

When Ethan screams loud, hoping Aries can hear him, a giant hand appears above Aries just as Fire leaves her. She ascends and the fire is being pulled from her chest, as Ethan tries to stop the giant but can't. She then falls back to the ground, when the giant laughs in joy.

Ethan then witnesses a painful sight when Aries turns into dust and flies away. As he is screaming, the giant punches the ground, leaving an explosion to blow out the field and other planets.

Ethan's eyes then return to their normal colour as he breathes heavily, gasping for air. 'What's wrong? What did you see?' Asked Thomas as Ethan stands up and says, 'I... I saw Aries. She was being defeated by some giant who could take her power and destroy planets.'

Ethan then cries as Thomas and Scott hug him. 'I just wish I could be there for it happens. Be there before she battles him,' said Ethan when he is shocked to see a portal right in front of him.

'Uh… Guys, look!' he says, Thomas and Scott looking at the portal and can't believe that it just appeared. 'How did it appear and where do we want to go?' Thomas said as Ethan made his way to the portal. 'It doesn't matter. Let's go and save Aries,' He said, entering the portal as they followed him.

Cithadel went flying as she crashed into the cage of the prison, injuring her arm. Tadine then runs towards the guard and jumps at his face, whispering the voices to hypnotise the guard but it immediately grabbed him and threw him to the ground, opening a hole.

The guard swapped both of his hands, punching Tadine until he heard him beg to leave. The guard took them and threw them in a cell and Cithadel began to cry.

'Now we'll never help my sister,' she said, punching the wall. Tadine knew the only way for them to stop the guard was to send him to another universe. Being stuck in the prison meant they would have to attack from there.

'I have a plan,' Tadine said, whispering into Cithadel'S ear. She then started to memorise all the memories she had with her sister. All the fun and bad times. The laughs and the cries. With all of them combined, she held a fist and screamed so loud the whole planet was shaking.

The guard tried to attack her but he was going backwards because of the wind wave Cithadel was sending. When Tadine saw that he was about to fall, he focused his energy and opened a huge portal to an unknown black hole.

As the guard fell, Tadine was finding it difficult to close the portal as the black hole began to absorb the prisoners. There were screams and Cithadel begged Tadine to close it. 'I can't. It's too powerful,' he said as Cithadel heard her sister scream for help when she immediately grabbed his hand and told him to push hard.

Tadine then screamed as the portal was closing bit by bit. Just when Cithadel's sister was about to be absorbed, he fell to his knees and the portal shut immediately.

Breathing heavily, Tadine created a portal to the prison cell Cithadel's sister was in and Cithadel didn't waste time as she ran to her and hugged her.

Cithadel felt so good as she felt the pale skin of Poean. She then kissed her on her forehead, telling her how much she missed her and loved her.

Just as Poean was about to say something, Tadine made her eyes black and she went behind him. 'What are you doing?' Cithadel asked.

'Simple, I'm taking your sister to my planet so she can create my universe. See you soon,' he said as Cithadel got so upset she tried to scream but from shouting at the guard, her voice vocal was damaged. 'What-' 'Oh yeah, I made you scream so you couldn't stop me from kidnapping your sister. I could have obviously stopped the guard on my own but I knew you would stop me later when I tried to take your sister... Too easy,' Said Tadine as he laughed.

Cithadel then tried to punch him but he looked into her eyes and possessed her. Tadine then opened a portal and let Cithadel and Poean go through as he laughed.

Goaub threw Princess Fire to the ground as she stood up and formed a shield around her and Aries. 'Cool staff, can I go now?' Aries said as Priances Fire looked at her, angrily. 'You don't get it, do you? You have to use the staff to stop Gouab before it's too late. Aries, you must use the staff to-' Gouab then destroyed the shield and grabbed Princess Fire as she dropped the staff.

He then made her ascend as he placed his hand in front of her face and absorbed her fire. She screamed as it felt like her flesh was being removed from her. After he took her fire, she fell face flat as Aries ran to her. 'Are you okay?' Aries asked. 'No, you must stop him. Please,' Princess Fire said as she closed her eyes and died.

As Aries screamed, Goaub didn't hesitate to take hers as she ascended and he placed his hand over her chest. The Fire was already being pulled from her as she screamed for mercy. Just as he was about to take her powers, Ethan blasted a light beam toward her, pushing him away from Aries. Scott then sent roots to his feet as they wrapped around his ankles and made him fall.

Aries fell in Ethan's hand as he felt the joy to see her. 'You're okay. I'm here,' Ethan said as she smiled and stood up. 'You guys have to stay back. This is my fight!' 'But Aries, you can't fight him alone,' Ethan said. 'I have to and I only can. You'll burn if you try. This is my Ultimate Battle, I have to end this. Now!' She said, sending them far from her in a shield.

MOMENTS LATER...

Aries tried but could not stand up as Goaub laughed at her. 'You taught you could stop him even though Princess Fireball couldn't... WOW!' He said, bursting into laughter.

Goaub then grabbed Aries and began slamming her against the ground, until she weeped for mercy. 'It's time to end this,' Goaub said as Aries levitated and he placed his hand over her chest, absorbing her fire.

Ethan saw this and screamed that he stopped but he couldn't hear him. Ethan then fell to his knees. He knew that he was going to lose another teammate and this time it was the girl he loved.

Aries then had flashbacks of all the time she spent with the Dimensions. Them being there for her. Having a best friend who was a girl and who could actually speak. Having her first crush. She knew that she didn't need her family because they already were the family she needed and they couldn't lose her.

While her fire was being absorbed, she looked toward the staff and focused her energy on it. It moved a bit but she knew she had to use all her energy. All her love and fire.

When she blinked, it appeared in her hands and tapped Goaub with it, sending him to clash on her ground. Aries then landed as she closed her eyes and lifted the staff ten centimetres above her foot. All the Fire on the planet was absorbed into the staff as she opened her eyes and tapped the ground, sending a huge explosion.

When the smoke cleared up, Aries was wrapped around a red-orange-yellow flame with TEACS on her right. Goaub was surprised. She truly was the chosen fire element.

TEACS then flew to Goaub and he blasted fire from his mouth to him while Aries began to send huge fireballs with rocks in them. Goaub then jumped as he held TEACS and punched him so hard to transform back to his little form. Aries screamed in pain.

She flew to Goaub as she waved the staff and sent lava balls to him as he screamed in pain. She then tapped the staff on him, removing his arms and legs from his body. Goaub then huffed as the fire smoke actually burned a bit of Aries's skin as he hit her with his head, sending her to the ground, burnt.

Aries was weak. No matter how much she could try to stop him, he always had a trick up his sleeve. She heard someone grunt in pain when she eyes Ethan. 'What are you doing here?' she asked, standing up. 'Aries, you must stop him. You're the only one who can. You are the chosen fire element. These people need you to stop him. I need you to stop him,' Ethan said, grunting in pain. 'But I can't. He's too strong,' Aries said, looking at Goaub still destroying the fire planet with his head and chest.

'You can do it. You wanna why, because I TRUST you. You've got this!' Ethan said when Aries eyed Goaub and came up with a plan.

She then waved the wand as she threw it in the air and opened a fire portal that lead to the hottest fire planet of them all, The sun.

She flew to him and called his name when he immediately looked at her and began to chase her. When he was near the portal, Aries went behind him and fire blasted him from his rear end, pushing him into the portal as she followed.

Ethan then told her not to go as they eyes each other and she went into the portal. Thomas and Scott then took him back to the shield as he screamed that she came back.

When Aries tried to blast Goaub, he somehow grew his body parts and blasted at her and so did she. They were at a tie. The person who felt weak would be sent to the sun and burnt away when Aries couldn't hold up.

'I don't know what they saw in you. You're just a typical girl with fire abilities. You don't have the flame to stop me. My plan for fire domination will be a piece of cake with a cherry on top,' Goaub said as Aries was falling weak and couldn't hold her fire blast.

Just as she was about to give up, she saw the staff floating around and immediately knew that she stopped so far, she did have the power to complete it. She was the one who end Gouab once and for all.

She then held the staff with one hand and closed her eyes, creating the most powerful fireball with the staff in it. When she let go, she was able to avoid his blast as she pushed back and threw the staff to Goaub.

'You really think the staff is going to-' and when it touched him, it exploded, pushing him to the sun as Goaub burnt away into Ash.

Aries was so weak she couldn't move and it was bad because she was drifting towards the sun, which could also end her life.

Minutes passed by and there was no sign of Aries when Ethan screamed in pain. He couldn't believe it. She was gone. He lost not one but two of the girls they had.

Ethan then started to punch the ground when Thomas picked him up and hugged him which made him cry more. Ethan wiped his tears and looked towards the portal. 'I have to have trust. I know she will be back... I trust her,' he said as they all eyed the portal which was closing.

She had so many memories, so many flashbacks but as Aries faced the other way, she had seen a light that was attracting her and forcing her to come. When she was about to go, she saw him. She saw Ethan as he said. 'Do you love me?' 'Yes, I always will.' 'Then don't go. Come back to me. Come... Back... To... ME..' he said as Aries decided if she was going to let go or go back.

Without hesitation, she made her decision.

The portal closed and Ethan fell to his knees, crying in pain and regret. Thomas and Scott tried but they couldn't as they let out little drops of tears. When the next portal appeared, Ethan stood up and walked over just as they heard a voice. As they turned around, they eyed her. They were happy and surprised.

Ethan ran to her and hugged so hard he didn't want to let go. 'Okay, Ethan, you're hurting me,' she said as he let go. 'I taught I'd lose you.' 'But you still trusted me and I returned. Now, let's go and find Clementine,' she said as they wiped their tears and entered the next portal.

As they placed their foot back on the ground, Poean redesigned Tadum and created two more planets as Tadine laughed in joy. Poean then made replicas of guards and old power pupils that were defeated by the Dimensions. Tadine was happy as he eyed a part of his dream that he wanted. 'This is it. This is happening. My revolutionary galaxy!' he exclaimed.

Poean then created another person who was perfect to stop those who tries to intervene in the way of Tadines Galaxy.

Chapter 15

As they landed, Scott said, 'Mistical planet!' The Dimensions looked at him in wonder as a man appeared with a grin on his face. 'You don't look like you're from around here,' the voice said. The Dimensions searched the area and couldn't detect where the voice was coming from. 'There!' Aries yelled as a young man hit the ground. 'DIMENSIONS ASSEMBLE!' Ethan yelled as they charged towards him.

They stood in shock when he multiplied into five duplicates of him. They each ran for a Dimension as they attacked each other.

Ethan tried to attack with his beam-sword but lost when it passed through the boy and the duplicate was able to punch him, sending him a distance far from where they were. Aries formed fireballs as she took shots but when she stopped, the duplicate had disappeared and when she turned, it smacked her to the ground and threw her across.

Soon Thomas and Scott came flying towards Ethan and Aries as the boy's duplicates rounded up and went back to his original form.

'What is wrong with you?' Aries asked. 'There can only be one!' the boy said, grabbing Aries by her neck and choking her.

Ethan tried to stop him but the duplicates grabbed him, Thomas and Scott and choked them. 'Today is your endgame!' he chuckled.

Just when Ethan gave his last breath, a man with a wand arose and waved it saying, 'Reversemosis!' and the boy turned into a tree. The Dimensions fell to the ground as the man looked at Ethan with joy. 'I awaited your arrival, Mr. Reddy,' he said, leaving Ethan in uneasiness. 'Come on, now. If you stay here, you'll be the forger's lunch!' he said as the Dimensions stood up and walked right behind him.

'I'm sure you're wondering why you are here?' The man said. The Dimensions were scared as they witnessed unexplainable magic happen in front of them. 'Hello? I'm sure I'm not speaking to myself!' the man said as no one responded.

The man got furious. He then held his wand and created a hole that was absorbing everything when the Dimensions got scared and asked him to stop. 'Do you not know what I just asked? If you do, ANSWER ME!' He yelled as the wind pressure got higher and they were close to entering the hole. 'Okay! Yes, we want to know where we are!' Ethan said as they collapsed to the ground and everything went back to normal. 'There are no jokes, here. You have a battle and I must train you. I must make you find your inner light!' the man said as Ethan got filled with fear.

They arrived and were amazed at how large the area was. Filled with animals, creatures and parasites, it was paradise. As they walked near a dam, the man grabbed Ethan's hand and said, 'You know why I must train you.' 'I'm afraid, I do not sir!' 'You are to battle King Tadum and his serpents but be aware he has increased his abilities and no one, like you, stands a chance. Yet of course, I must train you to stand a chance,' the man said, waving his wand.

Ethan was scared and worried. Was he going to be the only one who could save Clementine? Where were his visions when he needed them? When Ethan faced the man, he ascended into mid-air and closed his eyes. All he could hear was, 'NEVER GIVE UP...'

A white light appeared as a girl ascended. Ethan stood in shock when he saw her. When he saw Clementine. He immediately ran towards her and hugged her. He couldn't believe she was with him, in his arms. Ethan then took a step back when she looked at him with anger. She then created a puff of smoke and blasted him a distance far from her. When he looked at her, she was walking as she grew taller and taller, to the point he couldn't see her head. Ethan stood up and created his beam-sword as he jumped when she tried to punch him with her fist. 'What has gotten into you?' he asked. She then somehow blasted smoke from her eyes which burned Ethan's arm and made him scream for pain.

Ethan looked into her eyes as he blinded her and immediately jumped on her arm, making his way towards her face. He knew the only way to end her was the neck. Before he could strike, she screamed and sent a noise wave, pushing Ethan far from her face. Ethan fell and rolled as she grabbed him and brought him towards her. 'You are the reason why he got me. You are the reason Tadine can rule the universe. You are the reason for all the troubles we've been facing. You are no hero but the villain in our lives. Because you are the problem,' she said, throwing Ethan to the ground.

Ethan was weak. It was as if the words had opened his heart and poked holes inside of them. At that point, he was too weak to move. Clementine then went to her normal size as she created her smoke-sword and aimed it at Ethan's head. 'Please, Clementine. Give me mercy!' Ethan pleaded. 'Unfortunately, I can't!' She said, bringing the sword above his head.

As the Dimensions looked at Ethan, they saw darkness surround him and Aries became worried. 'You! What's that smoke surrounding him?' 'I'm afraid that is what is going to end Ethan's life.' 'You can't do that! You need to stop this!' Aries argued. 'I can't, ma'am. This is his battle. I gave him a message and he must use it, otherwise, your friend will not live,' the man said, walking away.

Aries then held a fireball, sending it all the way to the man. He swiftly avoided it and waved his wand, placing Aries, Scott and Thomas in a bubble.'Get us out of here!' they screamed. 'No,' the man said as he walked away.

Ethan looked at Clementine as she brought the sword down, closing into his head. He then tried to face his head down but saw a light. He couldn't help but look towards it. He moved his head to the right and there he saw, Clementine. He then saw the rest of the Dimensions fighting alongside her against thousands of creatures as she and Ethan created a black hole and saved the planet they were on. Ethan knew what the light was. He knew what the man had said. He knew to never give up.

He immediately grabbed her sword and flipped Clementine which made her fall on her face. She instantly jumped and re-formed back to the gigantic self as Ethan held his hands together and threw a beam of light which pushed a step back. He then tried to aim for her chest but she rapidly grabbed onto him and started smashing him against the solid ground, repeatedly. When she left him, he fell to his knees as she went back to her normal size and kicked him with her knee to his face. Ethan fell flat on his back.

Never give up... He remembered. Ethan looked Clementine in the eye as he stood up. Aries was stunned when a bright light appeared on Ethan's forehead and the smoke disappeared. The bubble then popped as the man said, 'He finally listens!'

He then formed his sword and went back to back, battling with Clementine with her sword. Each time he was close to stabbing her, the more her defense mechanism clicked in and defended her. They soon gave up as they stood opposite sides of each other. Ethan knew there was no time to wait.

The whole area began to convulse as Aries and the rest of the Dimensions couldn't see Ethan anymore because of how bright the light had gotten. He then looked at her and looked towards his sword. He knew the only way through was the light. He acted as if he had fallen to his knees as she saw him and ran towards him. Waiting for the perfect moment, he saw her last footsteps as she convoluted her sword and he reflected his sword towards her eye, blinding her and then capturing her in his arms. When she looked down, she saw his sword had gone right through her chest.

'No matter how many times you blame me, I'm not giving up,' Ethan said as she screamed into dust and deceased. A light then moved fleetly as it stopped in front of Ethan and Clementine emerged. She then moved closer to him and said, 'I await for you and the team to rescue me,' as she touched his forehead and he came back to reality.

'Ethan, are you okay?' Aries asked as she hugged him. Ethan nodded as the man walked towards him and said, 'Light and Dark are different yet they are the most powerful thing when mixed!'

Ethan couldn't understand what this guy meant. He then asked him, 'Who are you?' 'I am Ebenzer,' Ebenzer replied. Before Ethan could ask another question, the portal arose and it led all the way to Kingdom Tadum. As they were about to leave, Ebenzer grabbed Ethan's hand and said, 'Brighter and Brighter, Lighter and Lighter. Glow,' as he turned around and walked away.

'His weird,' Thomas said as Ethan smiled. They then held each other's hand as they entered the portal.

Chapter 16

As Tadine placed the image of the girl on the floor, Citadel's sister held it and the image came to life. As it was born, Tadine commanded the girl to touch Cithadel and when she did, she lightened up. She immediately screams at Cithadel sending her to hit her back against the hard rock. Tadine laughed as he sensed the feeling of unwanted guests. He told the girl that her name was Touch and that with her abilities, she could absorb anybody's power and use it against them. 'Go and stop these unwanted guests, no matter what!' Tadine said as Touch screamed to the floor, forcing her to levitate.

When they arrived, Ethan's eyes immediately glowed and he fell to a battle scene. Looking around, he knew he was by the kingdom of Tadine. As he heard a yearning for help, he ran to the voice and stumbled upon Clementine who was holding on to life. He then looked into her eyes as she squeezed his hands and gave her last breath. He kept shaking her hoping she would move but she didn't. Ethan cried and screamed as he dropped Clementine. "You tried your best," Aries said as Ethan started breathing heavily.

His eyes turned back to normal and he breathed hard due to the vision. 'What's wrong?' Thomas asked. 'Clementine, I saw her and she didn't make it. I have to prevent that vision from happening,' Ethan said just as he was blasted with a fireball against the tree. Everyone then eyed Aries as touch appeared and fire blasted them all. Touch then jumps to Thomas, gaining his power and electric blasting the dimensions, giving them a shock. Before she could take Ethan's, Scott made a root shield that hovered over them. 'What the hell?' Aries said, angrily. 'It seemed Tadum knew we were here and sent a soldier.' 'Where did he get the power to make one?' 'I don't know but I have to stop him. You guys take care of her while I stop Tadine once and for all,' Ethan said as his beams blasted touch and ran all the way to the kingdom.

As Scott tried to send roots to Touch, she immediately used Thomas's electricity to shake them as she headed for Scott and got him too. She then made vines tie around the dimensions, locking them in their position as he fire-blasted them. Aching in pain, Touch then made roots wrap around her hand as fire lit upon the roots striking with electricity. 'This will finally end you dimensions once and for all. Say assemble,' Touch said as she waved the power ball in the air ready for impact.

As Ethan arrived, he was startled to hear a laugh behind him. 'I knew it was you,' Tadine said, forming a smoke sword. 'Why wouldn't you think so, after you took my friend's powers, you deserve to lose.' 'I don't think so,' Tadine said as he aimed his sword at Ethan's head but he blocked it with his beam sword as they clashed back to back. Tadine then tried to stab him but Ethan blocked it, as he kicked him in his chest dropping his sword. Ethan immediately used his sword to hit Tadine by his neck but Tadine swiftly avoided it and got his sword as he stomped his foot against the floor and sent Ethan sliding back.

Just as Tadine came flying to slice Ethan, Ethan quickly moved and cut Tadine's arm as he screamed in pain. Ethan stood in shock as Tadine grunted and blasted a puff of smoke which Ethan avoided by somehow turning into a ball. When he transformed back, Cithadel appeared behind him and screamed, making Ethan's ears sore as he made the whole room shine, blinding her with his light. Because he was distracted by Cithadel, Tadine popped up and injured Ethan's cheek as he punched him so hard he hit a hole in the ground. Struggling to stand up, Saliva was dripping from Ethan's mouth as Tadine jumped and smashed him against the ground, over and over again.

Finally, in his weak state, Tadine's eyes turn dark as the surrounding area turns to smoke just as Ethan falls and his eyes glow. Ethan then sees Cithadel and her sister get blown away as Touch screams at them. Tadine then tries to kill Touch in his new form as She combines all the powers she touched and jumps to him, clashing separating Clementine and Tadine as he screams in pain and a huge explosion occurs. Ethan then gets back to reality as Tadine has a smoke in his hands and he throws it to Ethan as it bombs and sends Ethan across the room. Tadine then makes black vines tie around Ethan, choking him and tightening around his stomach as Tadine laughs at Ethan's pain.

With the last bit of power, Scott makes roots tie around Touch's legs as she falls and the power ball lands right next to her. 'A-Aries, you're the only one powerful enough to stop her,' Scott said as Aries remembered how she stopped Gouab and saved the fire world. She then breathes normally trying to find that inner fire when

Touch stands up and in anger, throws the power ball which flies to the dimensions, ripping the ground as it passes through. Just before it could clash, Aries caught the ball and transformed into her Ultimate armor. Everyone was shocked as Touch tried to throw more and more fireballs but Aries avoided them and still managed to hold a heavy power ball. With anger, Aries screamed and fire erupted from the ground and sent Touch into the air Aries jumped in the air and said to Touch, 'You get what you give,' throwing the power ball to her as it exploded and pushed Aries back to the ground. The whole of Tadine convulses as Aries returns to her normal self. Standing up, they see Touch lying down unconscious as Scott uses the trees to make a log in which they enter and Thomas rolls them to the kingdom with his speed.

As the room shook, Ethan fell out of the chair he was in. He then stood up and tried to head out but Citadel caught him and screamed, making him fall to his knees. Tadine then saw him fall and laugh as he jumped all the way to Ethan. Tadine then grabbed Ethan by the neck, choking him just as Ethan formed a beam and threw it to Tadine's face as he screamed in pain. Ethan fell to his face, blood dripping from his nose. He tried to stand up but he couldn't and Tadine was pissed. Tadine then made his eyes turn dark as he formed his smoke sword and prepared to slice Ethan's head off just as the dimensions arrived and Aries blasted him back to his chair.

Scott immediately made a shield of roots as Tadine and Cithadel tried to break it down. 'Are you okay?' Aries asked as Ethan nodded his head and coughed. 'Uh, guys? I can't hold this shield for too long,' Scott said. 'What are we going to do? He's too powerful.' 'We can stop him. All we need is her,' Ethan said as he pointed to Touch.

'DIMENSIONS ASSEMBLE!' Ethan yelled as their powers revived, bursting the shield open. As they eyed Tadine, he smiled and looked at them as he closed his eyes. His legs started to grow and multiply into eight legs like a spider and in between them, he had wet tentacles as his body grew as well as his head. 'What in the creature is that?' Aries asked as Tadine laughed. 'You didn't think I wasn't ready for you to come back. I knew you wanted to save your friend so I gathered her powers and made myself, Tadine,' He said as used a tentacle to hit Ethan all the way to the wall.

Aries pinched Touch as she screamed so loud that Cithadel and her sister perished in Dust. Tadine then grabbed Aries, bringing her to him as he formed a fist and punched to the ground. Scott then made roots wrap his legs as he almost fell but he grew back in and out as he made the tentacles grip Scott and suffocate. Thomas then tried to run to Scott but Tadine made his eyes turn dark again and Thomas got stuck in black quicksand. Tadine then brought Ethan closer to him as he laughed, looking at Aries weak on the floor, Scott trying to breathe while a tentacle was suffocating him and Thomas who was slowly sinking in black quicksand.

'You were dumb to think that you could stop me,' Tadine said as he made the tentacles knot on Ethan's neck. Ethan's eyes then glowed and this time found himself back with Ebenzer. 'What are you doing, Ethan?' Ebenzer asked. 'I can't do this. The whole team is close to dying and Tadine is too powerful even after the training. I'm pathetic.' 'No, you're not. Remember what I told you, Ethan.' 'But I don't know what you said?' 'You need to listen more. Remember,' Ebenzer said as he disappeared.

Ethan tried his best, trying to remember but he couldn't until he saw Clementine. He then went closer to her as she said, 'Brighter and Brighter, Lighter and Lighter, Glow.' And Ethan returned to reality as his body began to lighten up. He then took a deep breath in and said the same thing Clementine said. 'Brighter and Brighter, Lighter and Lighter-'

His body became lighter than the sun and when he looked at Tadine and said, 'GLOW!' the whole planet of Tadine exploded, bursting from the inside of the planet, sending rocks across the universe. Everyone was either weak or unconscious as Tadine returned to his original form. Ethan stood up as he looked at Thomas and Thomas went running with Touch as she held the conclusive power ball mixed with all the abilities she touched and clashed against Tadine, separating him and Clementine.

When the explosion ended, Ethan instantly formed his beam sword and jumped so high, that he was landing in speed as he aimed for Tadum's chest and hit it. Tadum then yelled, 'NO!' as he exploded and sent Ethan to a rock as he hit his head. Everyone stood up as they headed to Clementine who was coughing. 'OMG! Clementine. It's so good to see you,' Aries said as she and the boys hugged Clementine. They all looked around and saw Ethan on the rock as they headed there. Aries then gave him a bit of heat as he woke up and also coughed some spit. 'Oh Thank God,' Aries said as she hugged him.

As soon as Ethan looked at Clementine, he hugged her so hard he couldn't believe he saved her. They all joined for a group hug as they smiled and chuckled. 'Thanks for saving me you guys. You're the best,' Clementine said as she smiled. As they were about to leave, Clementine then gasped as they looked at her and she told them that she couldn't feel her powers anymore. 'What do you mean?' Scott asked. She then tried turning the planet dark but nothing happened when Ethan's eyes glowed again and he saw Clementine's power head back to where they all got theirs, at the M. E.N.S.I.O.N building.

Ethan got back to reality and told them what he saw as a portal opened to Menia. 'Guess we're going back,' Aries said as they held each other's hand heading back to where it all started.

They then moved the rock out of the way as they saw the Dimensions head in a portal. They tried screaming for them but it closed and they were stuck in this broken planet. They then looked around and saw chaos as the person held a fist and said, 'One day, you're going to pay for what you did to me, Dimensions.'

Chapter 17

Walking through the portal, they couldn't believe what they were seeing. Buildings and cars were destroyed. This wasn't the city or world they had grown in, it was a total disaster. They walked deeper into the area, as a screeching sound appeared and they eyed a creature as tall as a bus with ten legs and teeth shaped like cones. It croaked and ran fast as Thomas said, 'A-a-a Ogg!' and they accelerated away from the creature. It was fast but before it could capture them, Clementine saw a building and made her way to it, following her was the rest of the group.

As they entered the building, Thomas and Scott were forced into a sack as the kidnappers went with them quietly, out of sight. Aries then looked around and wondered where they were when the three of them heard screaming across the building. They quickly head to the scene where they are faced with a girl screaming in fear against a monster that seemed dangerous moving closer to the girl, its mouth opening wide. Aries then made a fireball and threw it to the monster, injuring its eye. Ethan formed his beam sword and ran to the monster, jumping and stabbing it, slicing it from its head to the ground.

The monster then roared, opening into two. The little girl ran to Aries, jumping into her arms. 'Woah! You are heavy,' Aries said, trying to catch her breath. Ethan then heard movement when he made light appear in the room and saw not one but thousands of people either hungry, skinny, or weak. This made their hearts sore as the people tried to avoid the light.'What happened here?' Clementine asked as one of the people stood up, walked over to her and said, 'After the heroes had left to find Dr Robertson, more and more of the creatures came out of the portal and destroyed half of Menia.

It was total destruction as millions of Menians were dying by the minute. We tried to fight for ourselves but failed. We also tried to fight-' she said, coughing.'-them so we could eat but it was too alien and killed half of the survivors. We've tried living here of little bits and pieces of food while others were dying but what's worse- is that The Other Side might be planning to make the whole of Menia their own.''Wait, who is the other side?''We don't know but there are posters that appear to be appealing when speaking about them. We at this point have given up on life,' the woman said as she went and sat down.

Aries, Ethan and Clementine then huddled up as they couldn't believe what they had heard. How did this happen while they were gone? Aries then dropped a tear as fire lit on the floor. 'Sorry,' she said. Ethan then made his way to them and asked what happened to the leader of the M.E.N.S.I.O.N? and of them answered, 'They disappeared out of the blue. Once the attacks got worse, they couldn't handle the pressure of the chaos. So we presume they took the mayor and fled, leaving us the people to suffer in pain.'

Ethan walked to the corner, as he let out a flood of tears.

As they removed the sacks, Scott and Thomas tried to catch their breath when a group of people surrounded them, wearing a Grey mask. 'When it couldn't get worse,' Scott said as a man in a black suit made his way to the both of them. 'Well... What a delight to have two offerings to the "beasts" that await its sacrifice,' he said as his minions grabbed Thomas and Scott, dragging them out of the factory.

Thomas and Scott pleaded for mercy, hoping they would understand but the leader and his men left them there. They then heard the brawl of the creatures as it saw them and all of those monsters ran towards them. Thomas and Scott screamed for help but the leader smiled looking at them. Thomas was scared. He didn't know what to do.

His powers started to react as he closed his eyes and the electricity made its way through the lines, striking the creatures as they exploded. The leader was shocked. He couldn't believe what he saw. He immediately commanded his men to go and bring the both of them back, locking them in a secure room.

Thomas and Scott, finally seeing each other held hands but were disturbed when the leader entered the premises, looking rather happy. 'I must say, you two are very unique but yet you can be useful. We want the whole of Menia to be ours and with our abilities, I will destroy or end anything that comes in my way. The other side will be on everyone's wide,' He said, almost walking away when Scott said, 'Oh no, what if he finds Clementine's powers locked back at the M.E.N.S.I.O.N building.'

The leader then looked at his men as they took Scott and Thomas, making their way to the building.

Clementine then asks the group if they perhaps know where the Menia building is and they answer, 'It's not far but only a couple walks ahead.' 'Thanks. We'll be back to help you all,' She said as the three of them made their way to the building.

They arrived but we flummoxed at the view of MENSION. It had been destroyed and also filled with hungry creatures lurking for food. They moved swiftly and quietly, as they had made it to the building, Clementine burst with joy, eyeing her powers. They glowed from the distance but she was hesitant. Clementine ran as fast as she could but was stopped by roots which grabbed her by her ankle and pulled her to the ground. They were surprised. They couldn't believe what they saw.

In the distance, they heard a laugh as he made his way to them. 'I must say, they look beautiful from the distance, don't you agree.' 'DON'T YOU DARE TOUCH THEM!' Clementine yelled. 'Too late!' he said, placing his hands towards the powers and they entered him, turning his veins dark and his eyes as well. He screamed and an explosion of darkness took over the room.

He was floating as the laugh he was giving became strong. He introduced himself as Sprit as he whispered a spell and the building began to collapse. Aries instantly morphed into her Ultimate form as she grabbed Ethan and Aries, escaping from the event. Scott made roots shield around the rest of the people as Spirit said, 'Let the war begin.'

CHAPTER 18

When everything relaxed, Scott removed the roots and the hostages ran away. They searched for an exit and when they found one, a hostage had been held by a rock and it seemed the building was still collapsing as Thomas used his speed to rescue them. By the time Thomas got the hostage, the rest of the rocks had fallen and they couldn't escape.

'THOMAS!' Scott shouted as dust flew past him and the hostages. The hostages then helped Scott up as electricity charged through the atmosphere and by the time Scott looked back, Thomas had made it. They all cheered as Scott ran and hugged Thomas. During the moment, there was croaking as a creature had made its way to them. 'Oh no,' Thomas said.

As Aries saw a clear opening, she landed and dropped Ethan and Clementine as she morphed back into her normal self. 'What the flip!' Ethan exclaimed as Aries ran for the fig tree and ate all the figs. Clementine and Ethan then stared at her as she said, 'What? I'm hungry!' 'We're not looking at you, we're looking at that,'

Ethan said as he walked in front of the tree and The M.E.N.S.I.O.N. building caught their eye.

They ran as fast as they could until Ethan fell and his eyes glowed. He fell into The M.E.N.S.I.O.N building but it wasn't destroyed as a scientist ran past him and chased for a room. The scientists had then placed a tape into a microwave as the leader of The M.E.N.S.I.O.N called them to attend to something important. As Ethan tried to touch the microwave, he began floating as he got back to reality and awoke to Aries and Clementine shaking him.

'I'm awake!' he said as they stood back. They eyed the ruined building as Ethan said, 'There's a tape inside a microwave. I think we have to find it,' 'Is that what you saw?' 'Yeah, only one way to find out if it's true?' He said as they walked over there.

The building was horrible. There was leaking water dripping on the electrical cords as shockwaves made their way through the plugs. 'Any idea where the microwave is?' Clementine asked as Ethan looked up and saw it. 'How are we going to get up there?' Clementine asked as Aried morphed into her ultimate form and flew them to the floor. As she morphed back, Ethan instantly tried opening the microwave held him back as there was a cord connecting the machine to the bottom floor.

'Not sure if you noticed but there was water leaking on one of the electric wires. Do you want to get shocked?' Clementine said as Ethan replied, 'Well, how are we going to get the tape?' he asked as Clementine looked at him and held his hand towards it. Ethan's hands then blasted a light beam towards the microwave as it exploded and a hologram appeared on top of it. A woman was present and she said the following:

"To whoever is seeing this, M.E.N.S.I.O.N. has been destroyed, with no hope of being repaired. I'm recording this as I've found something so sinister that my life is expected to end today. The leader of The M.E.N.S.I.O.N. is not who you think he is, neither is the whole building. Scientists are supposed to discover or retain data and evidence to prove an understanding. But that's not the case. I've found out that Menia isn't our home. We aren't from this planet. We come from a planet that has food. Life. Water.

I don't know how we got here or how life was built here but I'm sure, we aren't brought here for a good purpose. Be careful, you may think that The M.E.N.S.I.O.N is over but it's far from over. Their plan has just begun and the first one is called Tadum,' The woman said as the hologram disappeared. They were speechless until Clementine said,' So are you telling me Tadum was part of The M.E.N.S.I.O.N?''I guess so. But the real question is, why?' Ethan said as Aries called them over.

'You think this will stop Spirit?' Aries asked as they grinned.

Scott immediately formed a barrier but realised that Ethan hadn't commanded their powers to activate as the creature broke down the barrier. The hostages ran as Scott formed a branch sword and attacked the creature. The creature roared as smacked Scott to the rock across while Thomas speed ran around it and when a tornado had formed, he jumped and shocked the creature. The creature then groaned and fell as Thomas ran to Scott and helped him up. When they turned around, more and more creatures appeared as Spirit made his way to them.

'It had to be you,' Thomas said as Spirit laughed. 'And you guys will be my score. If I don't get rid of your little brats, they might steal this power away from me,' 'It was never yours, you bit-'

Thomas said as Spirit made his mouth shut. The creatures then took both of them while the hostages hid away. One of them then coughed and Spirit stood still as he walked closer to hear again but when he heard an explosion, he jumped on the creature and made his way to the scene.

As Ethan and Clementine tried removing the weapon, they accidentally powered it up and it lit a blue light. 'What is this?' Clementine asked as Ethan breathed in and his eyes glowed white as he landed in a scene. Ethan saw Spirit laugh as Thomas and Scott's powers were being extracted from them. He saw the blue and green hue make its way into Spirit as he became more powerful. Ethan tried to stop what was happening but fell out of the vision and back to reality. 'Damn it!' he exclaimed as Clementine questioned what happened. 'Spirit is going to take Scott and Thomas's powers. We have to get moving,' 'But what about the weapon?' 'We'll have to take it with us,' Ethan said as Aries took a bite of the fig she had taken earlier and morphed into her ultimate self, flying away with Ethan, Clementine and the weapon.

When they arrived, one of the creatures from earlier attacked Aries as she morphed back. Ethan then formed his beam sword and sliced the creature's head in half as more came. 'You gotta be kidding me!' he said as he jumped and blasted the one that was chasing for him but didn't see the other as it grabbed him and hit him against the floor. Aries then formed two huge fireballs as she threw them at the creatures and they burned down. 'There's more coming,' Clementine said as one of the hostages caught Ethan's eyes and before he knew it, roots had tied around his legs and he fell. Aries tried to help him but someone super speeded around her and weakened her. When they saw Scott and Thomas, behind them was Spirit as extra creatures arrived.

'This is interesting. I wanted powers from these two dweebs but found out that Ethans might be the right one to rule over Menia,' Spirit said. Ethan tried forming a beam sword but Spirit somehow burned his arm and the sword disappeared. 'I wouldn't do that if I were you!' 'Why are you doing this? What will you gain!' Ethan exclaimed. 'Revenge. They left us here on this planet, all of us, to be eaten by these bloody monsters. We struggled to survive. Hoping that maybe, just maybe, they didn't forget about us and would return... But they didn't. Months had passed by and we were starving. I knew if I had more power, I would take back what's ours and hunt those who abandoned us!''But revenge won't solve anything. In the end, you'll get the Planet but the people would've died and then what? Who would you be getting revenge for?' Ethan said as Spirit stood quiet.

He was too furious to care about anything as Spirit connected the unknown device to Ethan and prepared to extract his power.' NO!' Ethan yelled as Spirit pulled the lever. As his powers were being pulled, Ethan knew what he had to do and he said, 'LIGHTER LIGHTER, BRIGHTER BRIGHTER, GLOW!' and the machine exploded sending everyone across. Ethan then stood up as he helped the rest of the Dimensions up but everyone stopped as Spirit laughed. 'You just don't get it. I can't be stopped and I'll never stop,' He said as he transmuted into a gigantic shadow.

The shadow then held all of the Dimensions in the air as the hostages below sucked in the shadow and choked to death. They tried fighting against this toxic air but it was rising and the Dimensions knew what would happen next. 'Once you're dead, your

powers will be mine!' Spirit said as Ethan had an idea. 'Mine...
That's it. Clementine, you need to claim your powers,' Ethan said,
trying to breathe. 'But how? It's in him.' 'You need to take them.
Even though they are in him, they don't belong to him. It's yours,
Clementine. And that's something that none of us possess. Take
back what's yours,' Ethan said as the mist covered them and all
the Dimensions held their breath.

Clementine understood what Ethan meant. She remembered all
the times she and her powers saved the day and stopped creatures
from harming her and her friends. She then opened her mouth
and breathed the air in. She didn't die. She looked around and saw
darkness as she moved towards the machine that extracts powers
and connects them to her. Clementine then took the wires and
when she saw Spirit, she said 'The darkness will always be mine,'
as she stabbed them into him.

The darkness then made its way through to Clementine but once
it felt her, all of it left Spirit and entered her, making blackness
move around her. When she opened her eyes, it was pitch black
and then she blinked and the whole of Menia burst into darkness,
killing every creature and Menian, including Spirit.

When she opened her eyes, she saw The Dimensions and ran to
hug them. They smiled and chuckled until Clementine took a step
back and they saw her beautifully designed black new dress. 'Wow.
I got an upgrade but not this cute,' Aries said as they laughed. The
hostages then came out of their hiding spot as they all ran around
The Dimensions and hugged them. The room was filled with joy
as a new portal opened up. Ethan then had an idea as he told the
hostages to come with him and he made a portal open the place
where they could inhabit. 'Even though we aren't allowed here, I

think it's perfect for you guys,' he said as a little one hugged him. As the little one was walking away, she gave a last stare at them and said, 'Find Dr Robertson and Save Menia, Damansion,' entering the portal.

They then held each other's hand as they walked through the portal together for the first time with their powers.

CHAPTER 19

'Disgusting!' the king said as he grabbed his daughter by her arm and threw her into a dark tunnel. She disobeyed them multiple times and this time they were pissed. 'Please, take me out of here. I'LL NEVER DO IT AGAIN!' She pleaded but they ignored her and closed the tunnel.

She looked around and heard whispers. She then tried to climb out but her lethargic manner led to her struggle. She screamed, screamed and screamed but no one listened. A dark ghost appeared in front of her and she connected her eyes with it. It then sniffed her and as it closed its eyes, it yelled "Open" and it entered her. More and more of these started entering her as her skin turned pitch black. Her eyes from milky white to maroon. Her brown hair fell off as she became completely bald. As she looked at the door, it melted off and she escaped.

While the king and his knights were still leaving, the girl took an opportunity to wipe them all out. They all yelled as the king fell to his knees and the girl faced him. 'Alyssa, what have you become,' He said as she replied, 'What you never wanted,' and she passed through him, melting his insides. Her sister and queen then saw what happened as they escaped but the queen wasn't fast enough. Alyssa had already made the spirits that possessed her to take over the planet as her sister ran and ran and ran.

When she finally stopped, she heard one of the spirits approaching and she panicked. A light then flashed in front of her as the girl saw a portal open up. Without hesitation, she jumped through and it closed.

As they walked through this planet, a young girl ran passed them as a creature that looked like an octopus chased after her. Ethan looked at the others as they nodded and he said, 'DIMENSIONS ASSEMBLE!' and they all glowed with their unique powers. Scott then used roots to tie around the creature as it fell. When Aries tried to burn it, it grabbed her and threw her across. Ethan then jumped and threw a beam sword as he sliced all the creature's legs off. Clementine then walked near it and touched its head as its whole body exploded. The girl instantly grabbed a stone and threw it at Clementine as she tried to run away. Scott then sighed as the roots wrapped around her and held her upright. 'We're not going to do anything to you,' Ethan said as she closed her eyes. The roots then left her as she ran to a corner and started eating the food she had stolen from the creature.

They felt pity for her as Ethan walked over. As he greeted her, she looked at him and turned away. As Ethan touched her shoulder, his eyes turned white and he fell into a scenery. He then saw the girl and another girl who looked just like her. As he tried to go closer, the other girl's eyes became pitch black and disappeared into nothing. Ethan then started breathing heavily as he got back to reality. Falling into Clemetines arms, Aries got jealous. 'He's fine,' She said as Clementine let go of her.

'I saw a girl that looked just like you but... Her eyes become dark and-' '-Alyssa,' the girl said as all of them looked at her. The girl then came clean as The Dimensions stood stunned. 'Well, I think it's best if we find a place to stay and sleep. One thing for sure, I'm hungry,' Clementine said as Scott winked at Thomas and said, 'We can... Look for food. I am ground so I can easily find food and Thomas's speed can get us food in seconds.' Scott said as Aries's nodded. Scott then jumped on Thomas and they both ran away.

'I tell you, those two,' Clementine said as they made their way to an abandoned place. They arrived at an unknown place and Thomas blushed. 'It's okay, I'll show you,' Scott said as he cupped his hand on Thomas's face. Thomas was pink-red. He then looked away as Scott brought his face closer. Just as their lips were about to touch, Scott's eyes turned dark and all of a sudden he pushed Thomas to the ground. He then made his roots tie around Thomas's neck as he begged for air. Thomas immediately started running as electricity formed and it shocked Scott. As Thomas tried to run, he felt his powers fading as It had been a long time since Ethan commanded their powers to activate. Scott then formed a knife made from rock and stabbed it into Thomas's leg.

Thomas yelled as Scott made the roots tie around him. 'Scott, what's wrong with you?' He asked. 'It's not him,' A girl's voice said as a dark shadow appeared. 'Where's Angela?' she asked as Thomas answered, 'I don't know who that is?' The girl then made a portal appear but it was as dark as the night. She then made Scott pull Thomas as they all entered it. The Dimensions were starving as Ethan's eyes glowed again. He saw Thomas and Scott being dragged into a portal as it closed behind. When he came back to reality, he yelled their names as Aries held his hand. 'What?' Clementine asked. 'Someone took Thomas and Scott. I don't know who it was but it was that same girl I saw when I touched you,' he said as the girl's eyes opened. 'I know where they went,' 'But how are we going to get there?' 'Ethan, your powers can make a portal,' 'Yeah, but it drains a lot of energy,' 'Do you want to lose Thomas and Scott just like how you almost lost Clementine,' Aries said as Ethan touched the girl as his eyes blasted energy that formed a portal. As he let go, he fell and both Clementine and Aries tried catching him. They then hung each of his arms around them as they made their way through the portal.

Upon arrival, they were instantly faced with a creature as that grabbed all three of them. Aries tried to morph into her ultimate form but the creature had drained them and Ethan was uncon-scious to activate their powers. The girl then looked at the creature as Clementine begged her for help. She didn't know what to do. She started to panic and ran away to hide. The Dimensions were close to dying as the girl started to hit her head multiple times. 'You... You can do this. You have to help them. 'THEY HELPED YOU' She said as she ran to the creature and stopped. It then looked at her and as they connected eyes, the creature let go of the Dimensions and walked away. Trying to catch their breath, Aries asked. 'How-How did you do... That?' but the girl stood silent. Clementine was pissed. This girl was weird and she was talking even though crazy sh*t just happened. 'Okay, that's enough. Who really are you and how the flip did you command that creature to let go of us?' But before the girl answered, someone appeared as they said, 'That's Angela and I'm her sister, Alyssa.' as she threw Thomas and Scott to them.

As Ethan woke up, he saw Alyssa and immediately yelled, 'DIMENSIONS ASSEMBLE!" as they attacked her. Ethan tried to beam blast her but Alyssa looked into his eyes and he fell to his knees. Aries still couldn't morph into her Ultimate form as Alyssa used her to blast Clementine but she was able to dodge the attack. Clementine then made her eyes black as Darkness started to invade the area but Alyssa was fast and made the spirits weaken her. As soon as Clementine fell, Alyssa made a hole in the ground and they all fell into the tunnel.

As Alyssa closed the tunnel with a cage, the whole room started closing in as the Dimensions were about to squash. They started to tear up as Ethan remembered what he saw when he first touched Angela. He then looked at Angela and said, 'Angela, you're the only one who can stop these things. Just like how... how you commanded the creature to stop, you... You can do it,' He said as Angela looked towards the walls. She then locked her eyes on them but they weren't stopping. The Dimensions immediately hurdled around each other as the walls were closing in. Angela then took a breath in and touched the walls as they stopped. She then asked them to stand back as she touched the ground and the whole tunnel exploded. The Dimensions escaped as the rest of the tunnel collapsed.

As Alyssa appeared, Angela jumped towards her and she fell. They then started fighting as the Dimensions wanted to help but Ethan held them back. 'It's between the both of them, not us,' he said. Their fight was powerful as Alyssa tried to weaken Angela but failed as Angela commanded things around her to attack Alyssa.

Alyssa then got pissed once she dripped blood. She immediately started to scream as everything turned dark and melted into guards. As Angela tried commanding the creatures to stop, she failed and they each injured her to till she couldn't get up. Alyssa laughed as she saw the pain in Angela's eyes.

As The Dimensions tried to intervene, the creatures got them and they fell weak. Ethan saw how Alyssa was going to end them all and he knew he couldn't let that happen so she crawled over to Angela and kissed her. As their lips touched, she saw everything. Everything he saw when he touched her. As they departed, Angela nodded at him as she stood up and walked over to Alyssa. The creatures kept weakening her but she didn't give up. As she got close to Alyssa, she gave her one look and went in. She hugged her. Alyssa was stunned as the warm love from Angela coated her. Alyssa tried to push her away but it was nice and as soon as Alyssa hugged her back, all the spirits left. The darkness and chaos left that planet as the creatures vanished. They then ascended as Ethan knew what was going to happen and just in time, a portal appeared. Without hesitation, he helped The Dimensions up and pulled each of them into the portal Ethan looked at Angela and she smiled back at him as the whole planet exploded, ending the both of them.

Arriving on another planet, they were speechless as Aries looked at Ethan in disgust. The planet they were on was empty no life, no matter, nothing. As Aries tried to talk to Ethan, an unknown person appeared from their behind and said, 'Welcome, Dimensions.'

Chapter 20

They stood still as they heard the greeting from behind. Ethan turned around and found himself facing this odd man. He wondered why he was all alone on this lonely planet.

'How are you, Dimensions?' 'How do you know us?' Ethan asked as the man took out a pamphlet. 'Well, you are the kids who took out King Tadum, right?' he said, showing Ethan the pamphlet. The pamphlet showed the five of them together as below it was written "The Unexpected Beings that took out King Tadine." he gave a little smile.

Ethan took a look at this man and the rest of the crew as well. 'Who are you?' 'I'm someone... Where did you guys come from?' 'Somewhere,' Aries said. The guy then smiled as he opened his hand to Ethan. Obliged, Ethan took his hand out and shook it with the man's hand as his eyes became dark. Ethan then froze as The crew looked at him suspiciously. As he collapsed, Clementine managed to grab him while the man laughed.

The man's eyes glowed as he looked at the Dimensions and carried on laughing.

The man opened his hand as one of Ethan's beam blasts appeared as he threw it and it clashed against the Dimensions, sending them to the ground. Aries stood up and got upset as she morphed into her Ultimate form. Flying towards him, Clementine pulled Ethan closer as she tried waking him up but he couldn't. She then checked his pulse as she felt it. 'He's alive, but we need to get safety, now!' 'Ohkay. I know what to do,' Thomas said as he began to run in circles.

Aries flew past the guy while he was throwing beam blasts. She faced him and screamed fire at him as he screamed in pain. Aries charged at him as the man in anger waited for her, holding a beam blast behind him. Before she could attack him, he punched the blast on her stomach, stealing her power and at the same time, sending her to the ground as she morphed back into her regular self.

He laughed louder as his eyes turned red. The man then punched the ground as fire erupted and injured Aries. Smashing against the soil, the man held a fireball close to Aries as she tried to stand up but fell back. He smiled as he aimed it at her head and before he could hurt her, Thomas swooped in and grabbed her, punching the old man as he fell to his knees. The tornado then took them from the scene as they traveled away from the old man. The man stood up and watched as he smiled.

As the tornado departed, the Dimensions flew to the ground, having a crash landing. Aries instantly got up and searched for food as she smelt insects beneath and started eating them. 'You know, if your ultimate form is causing you to be this hungry, you shouldn't become it,' Clementine said but Aries ignored her, devouring a handful of insects. Wiping her mouth, Aries walked over to Ethan as she saw his dark eyes and felt pain. 'Do you know what's wrong with him?' 'No. I don't know what that man did to him,' 'He must've done to him what he did to me, stole my power,' 'What do you mean, he's not Touch,' 'He's not but he's worse. When Touch took our powers, she copied them but this guy, this guy removed my power and left me with whatever was left,' Aries said as Clemen tine faced the ground.

The darkness of Ethan's eyes spread as his hands went from brown to dark. Each of the team tried waking him up but he didn't want to Thomas created static electricity with his feet and pressed them against Ethan but he still didn't wake up. They each kept screaming his name, hoping he would wake up as they felt their powers fade away.

He began breathing heavily as he looked around and saw darkness. Ethan stood up and heard a waterfall as he saw water drip down into the darkness. He felt something touch his shoulder as he turned around and saw this man who lost one of his eyes. 'Who-Who are you?' 'I'm Magnus,' the man said as he sat down. Ethan followed along but fell and injured his rear end. 'How are you doing that?' 'Simple, it's my head,' 'Why am I in your head?' 'I don't really know. I just need your whole team's power,' 'Why?' 'Because I need to get mine.

You see, kid, I'm one of those people who own a power, which I own is Magic. Unfortunately, my power or magic was taken away from me and now I have nothing. I am nothing,' 'So why do you want our power?' 'I don't want it, I need it. When I get your powers, I will use them to get my magic back and finish what I left unfinished,' the old man said as Ethan tried to ask one more question but the rook started to fill with water. Ethan began to float as he saw the old man sink. He panicked as the water was rising fast and he was close to drowning. He saw a little light beneath and realised that it was the only way out as he dipped and swam to it. The closer he got, the further it was as Ethan could feel his breath finishing. He then stopped as accidentally took a breath and sucked water. As he let out the last bubble, his eyes glowed white and he woke up back to reality.

'Ethan!' Aries yelled as she hugged him. Just as he was about to tell them what he saw, Magnus appeared as his laughter mocked the situation. 'Don't play hide and seek if it's easy for me to find you,' he said, punching the ground and causing smoke to appear, blurring the area. Ethan tried standing up but Clementine held him down as she said, 'You can't fight yet, you're still weak. Let us handle this,' she smiled and stood in front of the team, letting Ethan command their powers and their powers restored. Thomas ran around, removing the smoke as Aries transformed into her ultimate form, pissing Clementine off.

'Really?' 'It's my powers, not yours,' Aries said as she chased for Magnus. Magnus formed a fire blast as he sent one to Thomas. Aries grabbed him, flew up and crashed him against the ground as Scott made roots tie around him. As Clementine tried to let her darkness enter him, he sneaked a beam blast and sent her crashing to the ground. He then seized the opportunity to touch Scott as he removed all of Scott's powers. Aries tried to sneak from behind him but he made roots cover him as he jumped over and punched her with a fire blast. As she was on the ground, he beam blasted her, making sure she was weak and then toched her, removing all her powers as well.

Thomas came by fast and he punched Magnus in his face, leading to him bleeding from his nose. Upset, Magnus punched the ground again, sending explosions of fire until they hit Thomas and then used roots to tie around him as his beam blasted him and removed his powers as well. Before Clementine knew it, Magnus had already appeared behind her, removing all her powers, saying, 'Child's play, beam blasting her as well.

They were all weak as none of them could barely stand up. Magnus laughed as he punched the ground and roots with fire burst sending electricity into the air as darkness dripped down. He eyed all of them as he prepared to eliminate the entire team but Ethan saw what happened and in pain, began to cry. He tried picking himself up but he couldn't, seeing Magnus place his hand over Clementine's face and decided to give up as his whole body glowed and when he screamed, light overtook the planet, removing everything and anything. Magnus was lucky enough to escape and go through a portal but the rest of the planet wasn't.

The light began to fade away as each Dimension stood up and coughed. They immediately ran to Ethan, who again was frozen, but this time, there wasn't a pulse. The new portal opened behind them as Scott and Thomas carried Ethan. While she was walking, Clementine stepped on something and saw a key. She picked it up and saw how different it was as she placed it in her pocket and went with the rest through the portal.

CHAPTER 21

As they departed from that portal, the key began to rust and Clementine wondered what it was for. She eyed it's cornered, tilting it around. As she was going to take a closer look, Ethan's eyes glowed lighter as the team started to worry. 'Guys, we should really get him some help,' 'Yeah, Scott's right. He's deteriorating badly,' Aries said as the group picked him up and headed into his normal village.

In search of a doctor, a group of fiendish thieves caught the eye of the group. They stared at all their belongings as one caught his eye to the key Clementine had. 'That one, I say that one,' he told the others as they took siege.

The group placed Ethan in the middle as they surrounded him even if they were surrounded as well. 'Well, what do we have here?' 'A group of teens minding their own business,' Clementine said, but that thief laughed. They took out their weapons as the team began to worry. Not only was Ethan unable to command their powers but they did not have them at all. Clementine grabbed stones from the ground as she threw them at the group but they avoided them and injured her leg as she fell to her knees. 'AHH!" She exclaimed in pain. The rest of the group tried to fight back but the thieves were quick and experienced as in less than five minutes, they retrieved the key and made their way out.

'No!' Clementine yelled. Scott helped each member up as Aries looked at Clementine confused. 'So, what was that about?' 'We need that key. I found it after that guy made his escape. Now, it's gone,' she said as a drip of water fell on her. 'Rain' Thomas said as they searched for shelter to live in.

Upon entering the abandoned building, Clementine sat down and covered her face as she started weeping. Aries then joined her as she wrapped her hand around her. The rain increased as they found leaves and boxes and used them as warmth. Thomas watched the beautiful rain as he said, 'Not going to lie, I miss Ethan a lot. No matter what, he always gets us out of tough situations and with him not here, not even I know how we're going to survive,' and he walked next to Scott as they lay next to each other.

The Dimensions were hopeless as Ethan was frozen, Clementine lost the key that she found and even Thomas lost hope. They then fell asleep as the rain mocked the situation.

Opening her eyes, Aries heard the wonderful birds chirp as her hunger got to her, after all, she didn't eat when he transformed back into her normal self. She instantly tried to aim but failed as her hunger got stronger. She then climbed on the tree and braced for impact, jumping on the nest and capturing the bird and its three eggs. She immediately started a fire and ate away. As the rest of the team woke up, smoke burst into the atmosphere as Aries gave a loud burp and before they knew it, they lost consciousness.

'Hahaha,' Aries laughed as Clementine woke up. She eyed Aries devouring the food the anonymous man had prepared for the whole group. Scott tried to take his food but she almost burnt his hand as she swallowed it all. Clementine started breathing heavily when she couldn't see Ethan. 'Don't worry, he's okay,' the old man said as he opened his hand to her. She stood up and ignored him as she asked where he was. 'He's in my basement. I would suggest you come with me as there's something you have to do,' he said, leaving Clementine behind him.

She found him lying on a medical bed as the monitor measured his heartbeats. 'His still alive but there's something in there that's causing him not to wake up. Like a barrier or door,' that man said as he checked on Ethan's eyes. 'What do you suppose we do?' 'Well, I tried everyone else who could help but I'm afraid none of them were of assistance except you. You might be able to enter his mind and help him escape from whatever is happening in there,' he said as she walked over to him.

Clementine was worried. She didn't want to enter the mind of Ethan but knew it was the only way as she held his hand. The old man smiled as he began connecting wires from Ethan and Clementine. 'Perfect. All you have to do now is… Kiss,' the man said as she paused. She couldn't kiss him, since he is liked- the old man forced them to kiss.

Her eyes glowed as Clementine found herself falling and falling until she landed and hurt her nose. 'Oh, F*ck,' she said as Ethan helped her up. As he reached his hand to her, Tadum came out of nowhere and tackled him to the ground. In shock, Clementine ran behind whatever there was to hide. Ethan held him back as he tried to eat him.

Clementine then jumped on his head as she covered his eyes. Ethan then formed a beam blast and cut through Tadine as he exploded. Clementine was shocked as Ethan ran and hugged her. 'Thank God, you're here. I need your help,' 'I'm just glad you're okay. We've been worried. You're completely frozen,' 'I know, it's because that door is locked but I don't know where I'll get the key,' Ethan said as Clementine finally realised what it was for.

Before she could say anything, Speedos came running as Ethan could beam blast them all. 'This way,' he said as Clementine followed. They arrived in front of two doors, one was open and the other was locked. Clementine knew that that Key was meant for that door as they resembled the same keyhole. 'I know how to get the Key,' she said as she kissed Ethan.

Clementine immediately ran for the team as to her surprise Aries was in her ultimate form. 'What? How?' she asked. 'It seems my ultimate form wasn't given to me by The M.E.N.S.I.O.N so they aren't retractable nor are they controlled by Ethan. I told you, they are my powers,' she said, flying around the place. Clementine was irritated and happy at the same time, but she got a good idea as she grabbed Aries's attention. 'The key, we have to go get from those theifs. I know-' '-Sure, come on,' Aries said as she grabbed Clementine and flew away from the team.

Landing, Clementine told Aries her idea as she made her way inside the thief's building. On the other hand, Aries smelt something delicious as her stomach rumbled. She eyed three delicious snacks that looked like fries but she didn't care, she was starving. Clementine entered the factory as the thieves turned around and looked at her. She then started to walk like a model as she rubbed her breasts together. 'Say boys, I know we got off the wrong foot but I really need those keys,' she said, licking her lips. The boys were enticed as they handed over the key

She couldn't believe it actually worked as she tried to go back to Aries but one of them stood behind her.'Where are you going?' he said as he touched her breast. In defense, Clementine smacked the boy as he fell to the floor. The rest of the group stood up and aimed their weapons at her. 'You're sexy but we're not going to allow you to attack one of our crew,' he said as he took a shot at Clementine. She was able to avoid it and hide behind something but the shots increased as they surrounded her.

The youngest held his firearm at her as he blew her a kiss and took the shot but luckily Aries came flying in as she picked Clementine up and made an escape. The boys were pissed as they whistled and a giant bird came, helping them follow after Clementine and Aries. 'Crud! What are we going to do?' Clementine asked as the shot almost hit her ear. 'Get to Ethan as fast as we can,' Aries said as she flew deep down. The bird couldn't fly through what looked like a forest as Aries maneuvered the turns well. As she saw a waterfall, she wrapped her arms around Clementine and flew right in it as the bird stopped and hawked.

Passing through, they were near the place as one of the thieves jumped on Aries and tried punching Clementine. Aries then flew upside down as Clementine fell off and she crash-landed with them across the place. Clementine quickly stood up and ran as the rest of them were catching up. 'Thieves!' She yelled as the old man, Scott and Thomas grabbed weapons and went to help Aries.

When she entered the room, real speedos ran passed her as she saw Ethan ascend in mid-air with his body glowing. She grabbed the nearest chair and climbed it as she cupped Ethan's face and kissed him. Opening her eyes, she looked to her feet and saw water arise as Ethan tried closing the open door. 'What happened?' she asked as he replied, 'When you left, I couldn't handle the speedos, so they went through this door and escaped but then water started overflowing and I think I'm going to drown unless I don't close it,' trying his best to shut the door.

She showed him the key as Ethan held it and the water flooded the room. Holding their breath, Ethan swam to the door as he was close to opening it but a Speedo grabbed his leg and pulled him towards itself. Clementine swam as fast as she could as she needed to breathe but the whole room was filled to th e brim. She then used the key to stab the speedo as she accidentally breathed in and swallowed water. Ethan pushed through the water as the pressure was pulling him away. Just as he entered the key, he breathed in and swallowed water.

His body started to fall weak as he tried pushing the keylock. As he turned it, he let go and the door swung open. All the water gushed out as Clementine woke up back to reality and the speedos disappeared. Ethan then landed in her arms as his eyes glowed and a portal appeared. The rest of the team arrived as Aries was back to her normal self and the others were injured. 'In the portal, NOW!' Clementine commanded as they went through and it closed after Scott pulled the old man through.

Ethan stood up, coughing as he heard the gang gasp. When he took a look, total destruction overflowed the planet they were on as smoke filled the air and screams echoed. 'Oh my,' the old man said as Ethan started to feel dizzy and fell to the ground.

Epilogue

Earlier

    Arriving on the planet, Magnus had one motive as he made his way to the building ahead. The guards in front prepared for the attack while Magnus walked slowly, laughing. His eyes became dark, making the ground rise just as the guards aimed fire. He jumped, throwing fireballs towards them, burning one of them to the ground. The other alerted the rest without noticing Magnus coming in with a beam blast to his face. He instantly ran, over-hearing the footsteps of the other guards through the vents.

    Finding the room, he entered it to the surprise of the guards at his siege. He chuckled looking at the red lasers pointing towards his neck. 'You don't want to do this,' he said, making his eyes turn dark. Shots everywhere, Magnus making roots burst from the ground as they clung to the guards and he screamed fire from his mouth, burning every one of them. The alarm went off, echoing the steps that were approaching him. Magnus quickly grabbed the key and got the exit, only to be ambushed by the whole army.

They began shooting at him, Magnus gaining the upper hand and using the ground to cover him. He looked at them all, punching the ground and injuring each one of them in front. As the rest moved closer, he exposed himself ascending in the air. Magnus winked and before they knew it, the planet from deep beneath exploded, shattering the buildings. Cries and screams overflowed the planet as he laughed and prepared to leave when a shining portal caught his eye and knew who it was. 'Great!' he said, sarcastically.

PRESENT

Ethan stood up, coughing as he heard the gang gasp. When he took a look, destruction took over the planet they were on as smoke filled the air and screams echoed. 'Oh my,' the old man said as Ethan started to feel dizzy and fell to the ground.

Aries started shaking him when Clementine saw Magnus in the air. 'Uhm, guys... I see him,' she said, Ethan woke up, coughing. They all stood closer, Ethan eyeing the enemy. 'His going to use the key to open a portal. We have to stop him,' 'Okay, but how? We have no powers, well, except Aries,' Clementine notified Ethan. Ethan didn't care as he ran to the destruction ahead of the team as they followed behind him.

Searching the premises, Ethan stopped, taking a look around when a whistle caught his attention. 'You know kid, your powers are meant for you. I tried taking them but they only gave me one... Beam blast. Can't wait to get them all,' Magnus said, appearing behind Ethan and dropping him to the ground. The team surrounded him and braced for impact as he used the roots to pull them to the walls. Aries morphed into her Ultimate form and tried battling Magnus but he ran past with speed, grabbing her hair and dragging her down. She grunted in pain, transforming back. Magnus laughed, preparing to take Ethan's powers just as they activated and his new ability, Illusion, filled the room with scenes they had been to. From The Loop Planet to Tadine, the team dropped from the roots as Magnus couldn't handle the Slideshow. He immediately grabbed the key and opened a portal when the old man pushed him to the ground, leaving for the key to roll away.

The old man tried to hurt Magnus but he froze and his head hurt. Magnus pushed him over, taking his key back from Clementine who tried stealing it. 'You know why your head is sore, brother,' Magnus stated, kicking his brother on his stomach. After the grunt, he laughed, walking through the portal. 'NO!,' Clementine yelled, Magnus looking at her and continuing through as the portal closed behind him.

The Illusions stopped after he left with Ethan returning to reality. They helped him up as Aries held the old man by his arms. 'What the heck?' Ethan asked. 'Didn't you hear, he's Magnus's brother,' she said, pushing him to the wall. Almost asking him a question, the old man fell to the ground. 'Great, Aries. You killed him,' 'I didn't! I think,' she said. Ethan walked over to the man, lying next to him. 'I know how to get answers,' he said, touching his head.

He landed on a battlefield as The Guardians were fighting Magnus. Ethan saw through his brother's eyes, trying to help his brother. Magnus was close to destroying them as one of The Guardians held his leg, saying, 'Please, you have to stop your brother.' The old man didn't want to fret, seeing his brother hold the man with his eyes turning pitch black. He jumped towards him as he clashed his brother to the ground, letting one of The Guardians free. Magnus moaned in anger and pain, not noticing the strong man who stabbed him with a syringe and absorbed all his magic.

Magnus screamed in agony, begging him to stop but he didn't listen. After taking it all, the female flew into the air and smashed against Magnus, injuring his nose.

About to leave, Magnus started to cry as his brother placed his hand over his shoulder. Idiot, he said, touching his hand and pulling all his brother's powers. Too stunned to speak, Magnus punched him so hard, his eyes blurred as he tapped his head and all his memories of his life and journeys vanished into thin air. Magnus then created a portal and pushed his brother through. Ethan saw a glimpse of Magnus fighting The Guardians but he fell to the ground and before he knew it, the portal closed.

Ethan woke up, dripping saliva from his nose as he coughed it out. 'What did you see?' Scott asked, Ethan, trying to catch his breath. 'Not much but I think I know where Magnus is headed,' 'Okay, cool... But how are we going to get there?' Thomas questioned. 'Yeah, your powers are still trying to figure themselves out,' Clementine agreed. Ethan stood up and walked to the same place where Magnus escaped, tapping the ground and hoping that his powers would work. He didn't give up.

The old man woke up, eyeing the Dimensions when Aries's instinct pulled in and held his hands together behind his back. 'Can you stop? You'll kill him,' Clementine said, Thomas chuckled. 'My brother, he's going to destroy The Guardians,' the old man fretted. 'Who's The Guardians?' Thomas asked. 'They are an elite group of super alienatic creatures that not even you guys can stop them. They bring Justice to the Galaxy. They stopped my brother but I fear he's going to get revenge and if he finds his powers, you don't know what he can become,' the old man replied just as Ethan formed a portal. Sweat dripping down his head, he commanded that they go through, Thomas and Scott carrying the old man.

Magnus held his magic as it tried to escape from the tube it was in. He giggled, opening it and they plunged onto him whilst he screamed in joy. His veins turned dark before it used to showing the Dimensions abilities. Magnus then tried to merge his magic with their abilities but they rejected the merge as it caused him to bleed. He tried again but failed, punching the ground in anger. 'You know it won't work,' his brother said. Magnus turned over, seeing the team behind him. 'It will. They're appearance must be stopping the process,' 'Stop this brother. You know it won't end well,' 'I know... That's why I'm doing it,' Magnus said, making roots tie around the Dimensions.

Ethan nodded at the old man as he ran towards Magnus and jumped on his head. Repeatedly hitting it, Magnus screamed, making roots pull him down and fire blasting his brother to the ground. Aries tried to become her ultimate form but without food or energy, it refused as Magnus threw her across. He made darkness overtake the planet, making his way to Ethan. When the darkness vanished, Ethan found Magnus holding his hand about to pull his power just in time when his brother headlocked him, pulling him to the ground. They held hands when the old man whispered in his ear and all the Dimensions began to levitate. Their powers exited Magnus, entering them with a glow of their colour bursting from the ground.

They smiled with Thomas giving it a test drive. 'Yep. Their back,' he said.

Magnus was pissed.

After all that work, all those battles, betrayals and scheming he lost to four teens without powers and one who was figuring out their abilities. He screamed so loud the planet they were on and the surrounding planets convulsed. "Death," Magnus said as his brother departed from him and screamed, his skin boiling. The team was shocked, witnessing this as the old man burnt to dust. "Grow," Magnus said, growing taller and wider with extra legs and arms, The Dimensions moving back from him.

Magnus didn't laugh. He looked at them, so little as he said, "Spirits," and a dozen dark cloudy creatures emerged from the ground, speeding towards The Dimensions. "DIMENSIONS ASSEMBLE!' Commanded Ethan. They took charge as they battled against the creatures. Magnus was looking at one person and that was Ethan, desperately wanting his power. He howled, making his milky white eyes turn dark black. Magnus immediately started destroying planets while the team could hear the civilians scream.

'I have to stop him,' Aries said, morphing into her ultimate form. 'Here, you're going to need these,' Clementine said, handing over what looked like nuts. The spirits increased as the rest of them found themselves in a pickle. Aries blasted Magnus as he screeched in pain. She immediately flew to his eyes, burning them, and damaging his sight. Magnus snapped his fingers as stars began to fall. Aries avoided them, flying through but didn't see Magnus grabbing her and tossing her on a planet. He began punching the spot she landed, forcing her to morph back into her normal self.

After ending them all, the team saw how Magnus damaged Aries as They took flight. Scott made Roots push them up, landing them on him and attacked every side of his body. Thomas speeded around his head, giving him a headache while Clementine made fake mist enter his nose, damaging his nervous system, Scott made thorns from roses stab his feet, leading him to fall when Ethan formed a light sword and jumped, falling with him. About to stab Magnus in his heart, He said one more word and something huge occured. "O-Open," as a black hole appeared behind them.

Ethan felt his body get pulled back as he was about to enter it but a weak Aries pulled herself up and forced her form, swallowing the nuts and heading for Ethan. Grabbing him, they froze as Magnus said, "Stop," and everyone stood still except the black hole which was destroying and absorbing the planets near it. He then laughed as he said the spell and their powers began to collide with his

Let my greed igniteThe powers of they're fightDo the wrong, without the rightAnd make their abilities BECOME MY MIGHT

It was like the skin was being pulled from them as they saw the silhouette of their powers being extracted. Ethan knew this couldn't happen as he grunted in pain and saw his teammates cry actual tears as Magnus laughed. He grind his teeth together, screaming with his hands in a fist. At first, he looked crazy, but it worked as his powers were being pulled back to him. The rest of the crew saw what he was doing as they joined and theirs also was being pulled back. Ethan smiled as Magnus stopped laughing and kept reciting the spell.

'It's over, Magnus. It's our powers, not yours,' Ethan said, screaming louder. Magnus knew he couldn't let it happen, so he moved them closer to the black hole as their powers too became harder to hold back. 'No...' Ethan said, giving up. They all knew they weren't ready for this as Magnus began to glow with their abilities. But before he almost got them all, Clementine heard a voice.

Let the darkness free...

It said. She didn't know who it was or why it was saying that. The voice sounded familiar, she just couldn't put her head around who it was.

Clementine, save your friends and Let the darkness free...

It said, again. She saw how they were struggling to fight as their abilities were close to being gone forever. Clementine then knew she had to and said the words, "Let the darkness free," her powers bursting into bliss. Magnus covered his eyes as pitch-black smoke dropped from her eyes, moving down and stopping the procedure that Magnus created. He tried again but the darkness was so powerful, even his magic couldn't stop it. The crew landed on what was left of the Planet as they saw Clementine being taken over by the smoke.

Ethan knew what it was and knew it wasn't going to end well. 'CLEMENTINE, NO! DON'T LISTEN TO THEM!' but before he knew it, she had completely vanished. It was close to touching them as they panicked. 'Uhm... Guys, any ideas before we vanish as well,' Thomas asked. Ethan's eyes glowed and his hand moved in an upward motion as a light barrier covered them and all they could hear was nothing as the darkness wiped out everything around Clementine, including the black hole.

Aries, Scott and Thomas looked at Ethan, who was completely frozen, filled with light as they wondered what the hell just happened. As the barrier disappeared, they looked around and did not see Clementine anywhere. Ethan then woke up and a portal opened behind him as he rubbed his eyes. 'She's gone...' Aries said, crying. Thomas and Scott comforted her as Ethan looked at them and rolled his eyes.

'She did what she did. Now, we move on. We still have a mission and it's not going to finish itself,' He said, walking through the portal. The team was shocked as they couldn't believe what he said. Ethan wasn't sad or even worried, he just didn't care and they followed him to their next destination.

Clementine awoke to the sight of wonder as she found herself in a trapped tube. She saw the glass door and took a closer look, eyeing what she hadn't thought she'd seen in a long time. Scientist. They were jotting down notes when a mysterious figure made his way behind them. "Hello, Clementine," The head of the M.E.N.S.I.O.N said, smiling.